EXORCIZING THE DONALD

A METAFICTIONAL CHRONICLE OF EVIL

JOHN WAREHAM

EXORCIZING THE DONALD

by John Wareham

Cover design by Apollo Studios

Copyright 2024©Wareham Associates, Inc.

Published by **The Flatiron Press**

Library of Congress

ISBN 978-0-9795415-8-2

CIP data available from the publisher

PRAISE FOR WAREHAM'S WORK

"This 'what if' wrapped in layers of White House reality is a winner."
— Christian Science Monitor

"Invigorating—bold ideas and an almost cocky tone... a fresh and energized perspective."
—Library Journal

"Inspired—whimsical, philosophically savvy."
—Kirkus Reviews

"Stunning— an assured exploration of moral quandaries."
—Publishers Weekly

"Superb—wildly entertaining... a literary bonbon."
—New York Observer

"John Wareham was born shrewd."
—Business Week

"An astonishing original work that pushes the novelistic envelope within a literary framework."
—Malachy McCourt, Green Party Candidate for Governor of New York State

"Ranks among the finest novels..."
—New York Observer

"Eminently readable and wise... may well become a classic of its genre..."
—Harvard Business Review

"An amazing, literate... ruthlessly honest guide to life in the upper echelons of America."
—The Atlantic Journal

CAVEAT
Some characters are based on
real people in the public eye, and
fragments of their sentences may
have been drawn from conversations
within the public domain, and actual
research and insights into the nature
of evil. But all other characters
are fictional. Most of the settings
also exist, but what happens in
such places—or elsewhere in these
pages—is the work of the author's
imagination.

DEDICATION

To the achievers who invited me into their
lives, shared their travails and triumphs, and
taught me so much about the art, science,
and craft of leadership and prison reform.

*"If you want to test
a man's character
give him power."*
—Abraham Lincoln

EXORCIZING THE DONALD

CONTENTS

PART ONE

"Evil to him who evil thinks."
King Edward III

A CONFESSION

IF I LIVE FOR ETERNITY I WILL NEVER FORGET what I saw in the Mar-a-Lago chapel. My colleague was right there with me and says what happened was a manifestation of Satan. But I don't believe in evil. Well, to be honest, I'm a 'failed' Roman Catholic priest and I'm not sure of what I believe. So, on the issue of whether there are gods and devils, I might have to plead the Fifth. I guess these days I'm what might be called an agnostic. Unlike my Calvinist friend, Byrne Sage; he's a do-no-harm cleric who believes in a spiritual world where good mostly wars with evil. My other best friend, Jackson Wright, is a pragmatic sometime leadership guru who these days shares his gifts with maximum-security prison inmates. In just a moment I'll share the events that propelled us into a fateful meeting with Donald Trump, and then, apparently, with Satan himself. First, though, let me make a confession.

My name is Paul Gray and I joined the priesthood because I felt the so-called Hound of Heaven snapping at my heels to do what the Christians call God's work. While in the church, and this might seem a little unusual, I also completed a masters degree in psychology. My cardinal was happy with that. He felt it made me a more powerful priest.

Among other approaches, I happened upon 'existential psychology.' The key idea is that most human problems arise because we have only one existence. There's no afterlife, we're born and we die and that's it. So I prayed about what I should be doing with my life. In the end my head took over. The gray matter in my brain was very clear in saying that if I truly had a mission to save souls I was in the wrong place.

So I set up an appointment with my cardinal and told him I was leaving. He was very understanding. He said that given my intellect he was not surprised by my indecision and would give me all the time I needed to pray on the matter. But in any event, he said, such a choice would will need to be sanctioned by the Pope. Not on your life, I said. I've already made my decision. And I'm walking out those gates right now. And I did. In that moment I must have seemed confident and assured. But I was still more than a little confused, and still am, actually.

Bear that in mind when I tell you of our apparent confrontation with Lucifer and the astonishing aftermath—including, of course, the startling outcome of the 2024 Presidential election, and the fateful final decision of the Federal Judge at the November 26 'hush money' sentencing hearing. And, crucially, the site of the hitherto secret, hidden font of poison that incites the devilish behavior of Donald Trump. I'm sure you'll agree, the sting is in the tail.

I'm a trained listener with a great memory. I also discipline myself to keep a tidy journal of my key experiences, which I'm about to share with you right now. See what you make of it...

TRAGEDY TONIGHT

My cell phone rang. It was Jackson. I hit the answer button. "I'm sure you guys will be watching the debate tonight,"—I sensed a grin in his voice—"you know, the one between the old man and the con man."

"We'll be joining the world in tuning into that," I said.

"Great. So we'd be delighted if you Byrne could share the broadcast with us in our neck of the woods."

We exited the elevator, and stepped into the sparkling, twilight haven that had been converted from a hat factory into a landmark apartment building. Indirect lighting lit the abstract paintings on the white walls and seamlessly blended with the whitened oak floor. Four huge windows lined the wall that overlooked 21st Street, providing an unobstructed view of the spotlit crown of the Empire State building.

"Ah Paul!"—our host, who quit an illustrious career as coach to corporate teams, preferring to teach what he calls a development class for Rikers inmates, grabbed my hand and pulled me into a hug. "You're looking great."

"And trim indeed" said Margot, his ever-winsome lifetime inamorata. She air-kissed my cheek, did the same for Byrne, then stepped back and set her hand on her hips. "You guys could pass for handsome twins in your dark jackets, jeans, white shirts, and Gucci loafers." The fresh air was gently scented by the ample vase of cherry blossoms, magnolias, and tulips that Margot had perfectly arranged and centered on the glass coffee table, around three sides of which were the leather sofa and the four lounge chairs from which we'd view the large television screen on the far wall.

"You long-married guys are both looking as fair as ever, too," I said.

"If only!" said Jackson. He pressed back his shock of silver hair. "Margot says I look no older than fifty"—he grinned—"somedays sixty. But, as you both know, I'm about to join the ranks of the living dead." He shared a rueful grin. "Hey, wait!" he said. "Our other guests, whom you'll love by the way, are tapping at that front door button."

Margot jumped in. "So come seat yourselves on the sofa and pour yourselves a drink while Jackson waits for Hassan and Ashleigh to ride up in the elevator."

As always, Jackson and Margot's guests, whom Margot directed to sit in the two lounge chairs opposite the window, were intriguing. Hassan, a tall, rugged fellow with a salt-and-pepper complexion that matched his neatly cropped scalp, turned out to be a graduate of Jackson's Upstate New York prison program. Jackson and Hassan became friends. So much so that upon Hassan's release, perhaps on the understanding that it takes a thief to change a thief, Jackson included Hassan in his work with at-risk youth. Ashleigh, now in her trim and attractive sixties, used to direct prison programs. Byrne and I shared a knowing glance. Who but Jackson would think to invite this unconventional couple to dine with Byrne and me?

"How are things with you guys, then?" said Jackson. He sipped the ruby-red Shiraz in his glass.

It was a question for everyone.

"I'm worried," said Byrne, twisting his tumbler of Pellegrino.

"Given the current political situation it's pretty natural to worry," said Margot, smiling as she sampled her Chardonnay.

"I think we might all be worried that Trump will be 'the man,'" said Hassan.

"This debate between Biden and the Donald"—Jackson checked his watch—"which we'll see in just a minute, may end all speculation." said Jackson. "I published a profile of the

Donald in an earlier life—"

"—You wrote that piece twenty years ago when he got the job to star in *The Apprentice*," said Margot.

"I'd love a copy of that," I said.

"No problem," said Jackson. "I'll email you a PDF." He smiled. "Getting that gig was a defining moment for the Donald. He learned about the video camera and the red light atop it.

"Huh?" said Hassan.

"He figured out that when he kept the video camera focused on himself that the red light on the top of the camera never stopped blinking." As a photographer might, Jackson raised his palms, formed his fingers and thumbs into the shape of a viewfinder, and peered through it. "I see the Donald as playing one more role in yet another reality show of his own creation." He pointed both forefingers at me. "And, to be *the* star in any reality show you have *perform*. You learn to create roles and ruses that keep the camera focused on you. If you succeed, the red light is *always* alive and bright and blinking." He brushed back his silver hair. "The Donald used to play Terminator in *The Apprentice*. Nowadays he's playing Entertainer at his campaign rallies."

"Or Victim. He's good at that," said Hassan.

"And, in the role of Not-So-Crazy-Uncle he gives his followers permission to show their hatred," said Ashleigh.

"Right. And, if he could only get back to the Oval Office, the role that the Donald's hoping for is to gather an audience to applaud as the red eye gleams and he appends his Presidential signature to his pardon."

"That's quite a theory," I said.

"I've had awhile to think about it."

"So do you have a theory on Hillary lost to Trump?" said Margot.

"It might help to bear in mind," said Jackson, "that Hillary, wearing her suffragette white suit as her ardent followers celebrated her about to be revealed victory, pointed a forefinger to an apparently installed-for-the-evening glass ceiling that she was about to shatter."

"She won the popular vote by two million," said Margot.

"Yes. And on the very same November night when she was pointing to the dome, the Donald flew to Michigan, arriving shortly after midnight, where an hour or so later, he led a rally of some twenty-five thousand raving fans, all of whom probably voted for him when the sun came up."

"*That's* how he won the Electoral College?"

"He knew something that she didn't."

"Russian meddlers are fiendish devils," said Byrne.

"And the rest is history."

"But the Donald himself has two great qualities."

"He does?"

"Ignorance and cunning."

"Of course."

"And the sly side of him is terrified he'll wind up in a prison cell... and so, my hunch is that he's on a mission to stir yet another so-called popular uprising."

"His followers have the guns."

"So expect the unexpected?"

"Yes of course. The Devil looks after his own."

"Speaking of the Devil," said Jackson, pointing to the TV screen, "let me fill your glasses, for here comes his nemesis." We watched as Biden stepped shakily into the auditorium.

"He looks frail," said Margot.

"More so than ever," said Byrne. "And here's Trump."

"That's the Donald's Mafia-Don pose. He copied it, more aptly than he realizes, from the promo for the Kubrick movie *A Clockwork Orange*."

Mostly in silence, we stayed glued to the appalling hour-and-a-half CNN presentation. When it was over Jackson raised his eyebrows. "So…"

"It was sad," said Hassan, sipping his glass of Shiraz.

"Biden's performance was alarming," said Byrne. "He looked like a feeble old man who'd lost his way, and was too scared to ask anyone how to get back home."

"His stutter may have had a lot to do with that," said Jackson. "I know because I have one, too."

"*You* have a stutter?" said Ashleigh.

"It used to be a problem. But then like Biden I took up public speaking and debating—"

"—and won a ton of prizes," said Margot.

"And learned a lot." Jackson took a breath. "For someone like Biden, having to present a memorized formal script can be daunting. If he even thinks of stuttering he'll do exactly that. So stutterers scan ahead for gremlin words and phrases. Then they switch a word or phrase, or blur a name or sentence, or completely reframe a thought. But that can be a heavy load."

"And Trump *wanted* to trip him up," said Margot.

"So he scowled, ostentatiously crossed his arms, and tightened his lips," said Byrne.

"And mocked Biden's stutter," I said.

"Happily, in such moments, experienced stuttering public speakers forget to stutter. Instead we go off cue and banter with hostile members of the audience… Okay then, here's the thing about stutterers: the world comes at us differently. So we build big vocabularies, and, one way or another, we develop what others call 'a way with words.' We may not become smarter, but for sure we become more creative. Unhappily, however, there's no ultimate so-called cure for stuttering. It can return and often does, especially with the passing of the years, and in the kinds of pressure situations that used to bring out the best in us. One night it's there, and next day it's not."

"As we all saw," said Hassan.

"He looked as if he'd forgotten his lines," said Byrne.

"My take is that the pressure of having to respond to a nonstop litany of lies from a scowling, scoffing adversary threw him, like us, into a panic mode where he foresaw countless gremlin lines."

"So in trying to rearrange his memorized policy rebuttals, he merely looked like the ageist stereotype of a befuddled octogenarian?" I said.

"There are some tricks that only old dogs can learn," said Hassan.

"I guess," said Jackson. "So, though his stutter may bedevil Biden—and for sure he often looked out of it—he's also now a savvier and more creative negotiator. He's built a first-rate team and they've turned the disaster they inherited into the current world's most buoyant economy."

"The other takeaway," I said, "will surely be that Trump confirmed his status as an out and out liar—"

"—the fabrication he'll be remembered for is," Ashleigh sipped her Chardonnay, "'I never had, uh, sex, with, uh, a porn star.'"

"He never admitted that foible under oath," said Margot.

"Did he ever give *any* testimony under oath?" I asked

"The Donald runs from that," said Jackson. "He sees the risk of choosing to give testimony under oath as a choice between death by electrocution or being eaten by sharks. He said he'd *always* choose to risk dying by electrocution. The outcome of his Manhattan trial was his sinking ship. To dive into shark-infested water was to take the oath and succumb to the legal sharks."

We moved on to the CNN follow-up discussion. Panic was

the order of the day, but only for celebrated Democrat panelists. The two GOP strategists joined as one to sing the hymn, 'I Told You So.' The program ended, not with a bang but a whimper, and we adjusted our chairs back around the coffee table.

"So as I recall," said Jackson, "my original question to you guys was, how are things?"

"I'm getting used to my status as failed priest," I said.

"Don't believe him," said Byrne. "Sure, Paul was coerced to seize a pen and sign onto the celibate life. But his heart never did. His real mission was to be psychologist."

"Which he's always been," said Jackson.

"Wow! Psychology *and* religion," said Hassan.

"I pride myself on having an open mind," I said.

"Paul should have been an historian," said Byrne. He presented a happy smile. "Like my not always esteemed self."

"Paul says you specialize in religious history," said Jackson.

"I do indeed."

"Unlike me, you're also a committed Christian," I said.

"So what *are* you?" said Ashleigh.

"Maybe a pagan," I said.

"When the missionaries came to Africa they had the Bible and we had the land," said Hassan. "They said, 'Let us pray' so we shut our eyes. When we opened them we had the Bible and they had the land." He shot a grin. "So, given my history, I'd like to believe in something—"

"—Witch-Hunts seem popular these days—"

"—That may be truer than you realize," said Byrne.

"Do you actually believe in witches?" said Hassan.

"I believe in good deeds and evil deeds," said Byrne. "So I believe in witches who are evil-doers, and angelic witches who guide us to happy outcomes."

"They say the Devil looks after his own," said Hassan.

"Yes, but to perform his evil, Satan needs to take possession of a human person—"

"—who then becomes a devil," said Hassan.

"Or a witch," said Byrne.

"We all have to remember the eleventh commandment," said Hassan.

"'Thou shalt not question?'" said Ashleigh.

"I'm actually a Calvinist."

"Religion is important to you?" said Ashleigh.

"My heart says we're guilty of the good we don't do."

I jumped in. "But the world's not a nursery."

"Religion comforts lots of immoral people," said Jackson.

"My take is that religion is mostly a neurosis," I said. "Heaven's under our feet, not over our heads."

"I'm told that there's two wolves inside of us and they're always fighting," said Hassan. "One is darkness and despair, the other is light and hope. So which wolf wins?"

"The one you feed?" said Margot.

"Damn right!"

"But neither of those wolves can exist without the other."

"You don't believe in alternative-facts?" said Jackson.

"Or Fox News at all—the owner, Rupert Murdoch is pure evil surely," I said.

Jackson smiled. "He's not without charm."

"You might not say that if you met him," said Hassan.

"In fact I did."

"You met that old devil?!" said Byrne.

"Rupert arrived in New York shortly before I did. I'd never met him before, but he seemed a kindred spirit."

"And how did that work out?" I said.

"I stepped into the office he'd acquired from publishing scion Dorothy Schiff. He was wearing charcoal pinstripes, seated on what used to be Ms. Schiff's swivel throne. A 1950s black typewriter atop a matching credenza was behind him. He strolled around his desk, and shared an almost boyish smile. We sat in the twin guest chairs in front of his desk. 'Are you living in the city or suburbs?' he said. His curiosity was flattering. We talked about that for a while, then I confessed to being in awe of his acquiring both the London *Times* and the *New York Post*. I'll never forget what happened next. He beckoned me to look over a table laid with a huge range of *News Limited* publications and pointed his forefinger at a paper in the pile. 'That's the paper I'm most proud of,'—he dipped into the pile, pulled out a periodical, and held it aloft—'this one.' Yikes—*The Star*, a tabloid down-market copy of the *National Enquirer* was hanging from his fingers—"

"—He ultimately sold that rag," said Byrne.

"'Before I arrived here it didn't exist," said Rupert. 'And now it's making me fifty million dollars a year.' He glanced to his watch. 'So, what can I do for you?' I said I was hoping he might provide a reference confirming he was a client of my leadership firm. I detailed the assignments we'd handled then unfolded a draft reference I'd prepared. He took a quick look. 'No problem,' he said. Then he stepped behind his desk, plopped into his swivel chair, swung to face the typewriter, inserted a sheet of *News Limited* letterhead, and nimbly ratta-tatted my words. Then he plucked the missive, swung back, dropped the letterhead onto the desk, and fountain penned his confident signature in bronze blue ink. 'There it is then,' he said, smiling."

"So what did you learn?" I asked.

"That Rupert's a charming transactional leader. And, most importantly, money is his prime motivator—"

"—the *Post* gave him political influence," said Byrne. "But the profits of a supermarket rag made it possible."

"So, Fox fulfilled his dystopian dreams," I said.

"And the Devil hath power to assume a pleasing shape," said Byrne.

"And the Devil looks after his own," said Hassan.

"Better to conquer the inner Devil than win a thousand battles," said Byrne. "Every one of us is capable of wickedness."

"In my neck of the woods it's so hard to make a living that people often say, a man's gotta do what a man's gotta do."

"So they take the primrose path?" said Byrne.

"Maybe," said Hassan.

"Regardless of the consequences?" said Byrne.

"Sometimes the wisest course is to go with the flow." Hassan stroked his chin. "As I think you know, I spent serious time in some serious prisons. "So I happened to meet some great liars. And many of them were prison guards. So what I know is that supposedly good people can be better at lying than your average prison inmate."

"Maybe so," I said.

"If you doubt it, and if you're up for it," said Hassan, "I can bring you as my guest into the class I'm running in an upstate prison right now."

I didn't have to think about that. "If you can arrange it, I'm your man," I said.

"Everyone who promises too much is already on the road to perdition," said Byrne, with a smile.

"Speaking as a woman married to an upcoming elder," said Margot, "I've learned that the mind's pendulum swings between sense and nonsense, not right and wrong."

"It's what you *see* that matters. Sigmund Freud said that no mortal can keep a secret. If his lips are silent, he chatters with his fingertips; betrayal oozes out of him at every pore."

Byrne jumped in. "Carl Jung said the ultimate remedy for his late-life patients was to discover a religious outlook on life."

"Wow!" said Hassan. He shot a smile. "So this guy Carl, he's saying 'show me a sane man and I'll cure him for you.'"

We laughed at that. And, in our happy distraction, we forgot to worry about the rise and rise of Donald Trump.

But not for long.

In my dream that night, I was standing before a bearded, black-robed oracle. I was enraptured by his intelligence and by the confiding way he shared astonishing truths earnestly and wisely. Then his face dissolved into a dark looking glass. My head within that mirror was a video camera atop which a red light was blinking.

I awoke, pushed off the suffocating bed clothes, and stepped to the dark bedroom mercury. What I was expecting to see I do not know. Then, before sunrise, I lay wide awake on my pillow checking the news on my cell phone. The *New York Times* had issued an editorial urging Joe Biden to stand aside and make way for younger and more loquacious tongues. If the world is truly governed by gods in the form of good people, this unhappy debate between the Old Man and the Con Man might have sparked something good. Or maybe not? I did not know it then, but my life had taken a turn. And there would be no going back. I closed my eyes and fell back into the troubling sleep that can sometimes feel like an accomplice.

THE DONALD OF YORE

An email arrived. Seems Jackson made good on his word.

> As promised, I'm attaching a pdf of the article I
> wrote on the Donald way back some 20 years ago
> when NBC selected him to star in The Apprentice.

I opened the attachment, and read it carefully. And, given what happened later, I was glad I did.

HOW TO SPOT AND REFORM A GONNABEE
Instead of being stung by one
by Jackson Wright

What a world! At the apex of his narcissistic career, failing casino operator Donald Trump gets to fire aspiring tycoons—on 'reality' TV no less—for what he calls their failure to measure up to his demonstrably non-existent principles.

But here's the sixty-four thousand dollar question: How—really—can we spot such phonies before getting stung?

The key, of course, is to begin by suspecting every executive hailed as any kind of genius. Such praise typically conceals the proverbial can of worms. Trouble is, however, that such phonies become highly adept at cover-up and misdirection. So the most reliable prophylactic for the sophisticated hirer begins with an appreciation of the overall style of this particular genre of Brummugem.

Sigmund Freud first noted this narcissistic personality style. Michael Macoby, author of *The Gamesman*, calls such individuals "productive narcissists." Most of the time, however, this genre is embedded with the seeds of personal self-destruction. I call this torpedo variant, Gonnabee. Let's look—

Gonnabee

So badly do Gonnabees dream of becoming big shots that they can often gull you into believing they already are. Gonnabees look the part and play it to the hilt. Under pressure, however, they just don't have what it takes. Gonnabees are magnificent empty shells, all style and no substance, all hat and no cattle.

Few get as far as Trump, but all can be mesmerizing to watch—and nowhere more so than when you're the person who'll have to mop up after them.

I spend a lot of my time distinguishing among subspecies of the Gonnabee genre, and reporting their failings to clients who want me to say that some particular Gonnabee is destined to rise to the top of the company, and then lead it on to greatness. In fact, unless they receive professional help, most Gonnabees are fated for failure. Their true destiny is to go up like rockets and fall back like sticks.

When you meet a Gonnabee, your immediate impression is almost always of an aggressive go-getter, jaunty and confident to the point of arrogance. Gonnabees usually dress for where they hope to be going, and thus usually look like advertising photographs of top executives. However, a touch too much look-at-me dash—a gold wrist bracelet, a Rolex watch, a Gucci tag—usually gives them away.

Gonnabees spend their lives responding to a Western culture that exhorts people to "succeed," first by making money, then by flaunting it. Gonnabee thus aches to join the ranks of those who have overtly "made it," the so-called Big Shots.

Gonnabees learn—from self-help books and magazines, at inspirational seminars and meetings, on syndicated television shows and in training films—that "making it" is merely a matter of desire and dedication: that anyone who wants It badly enough can have It if only they will do "what It takes."

Gonnabee dreams are of success and celebrity, of money and fame, of status and power. They foresee penthouse offices, sensuous assistants, lush hotel suites, limousines with extravagant communication systems, finely paneled boardrooms, lavishly furnished private jets. They envision profiles in *Forbes*, portraits in *People*, maybe even the cover of *Time*. Gonnabees like to be around star athletes and dream of owning professional sports teams.

All such things mean vastly more to Gonnabees than whatever they're actually doing right now, for they never know the satisfaction of genuine job achievement. All they want is the status.

Understanding Gonnabee

The key to comprehending Gonnabees is to perceive that they are "reactive dependents," emotionally dependent people whose behavior is forever a reaction to that pervasive emotional ache. Thus, no matter their chronological age, Gonnabees are typically children trapped in emotional time warps, endlessly denying their dependence, endlessly seeking and failing to prove themselves serious adults.

In response to doting parents, Gonnabees become first-rate manipulators, alternately charming or fuming, to make a parent respond instantly to Gonnabee's every need or whim.

Like John De Lorean, who lived with his mother until he was twenty-nine, most Gonnabees also tend to be slow in leaving the nest, preferring the cocoon and comforts of the parental home to the gritty frustrations of the real world, and, of course, such cosseted upbringings further impair their emotional growth. Gonnabees thus always need people to stroke, sooth, and comfort them, to tell them what to think, to look after them.

For male Gonnabees, a series of wives—often one-time models or starlets—normally do the stroking. Advertising and television do the telling what to think, as in designer labels directing choice of clothing. Gonnabees usually live beyond their means and are often pledged to a credit-card company for the full amount of this year's anticipated bonus, sometimes much more.

Gonnabee emotional dependence is a source of constant frustration and anger, which they normally mask either with great charm, a macho pose, or both. The anger is often further exacerbated by an ever-growing sense of social inferiority, springing in many cases from feelings of having been born on the wrong side of the tracks. Gonnabees never realize that the tracks exist only in their own heads, of course, and so they often ache to get even with the world by beating those from the right side of town at their own silly games.

Gonnabees are quick to say, their voices usually rising a quaver as they do so, that "you've gotta believe in yourself." When wound up, they confide that their own success stems from their vision, their courage in believing in themselves, and the capacity to bring their dreams to fruition. The problem, however, is that what Gonnabees call positive thinking is what psychologists call "magical thinking." They want and need to believe that their own amazing thought processes in and of themselves can actually cause miracles to happen.

This kind of magical thinking, and the hunger and greed that fuel it, is carried over from childhood, when Gonnabees discovered they could get whatever they wanted by throwing a tantrum.

In reality, behind the macho mask, Gonnabees are invariably deeply negative thinkers, forever worried sick about ever making good on their grandiose goals. To ease the underlying pain, Gonnabees normally devote a great deal of time and effort to getting themselves noticed. Indeed, recognition is typically the entire raison d'etre of their lives. Gonnabees persuade the corporate public relations department to concoct and emit unrelenting releases in which they figure prominently. They aspire to become spokespeople, aligning their names with the corporate product or service, often to the point of figuring in the company's advertising, especially on television, until a general uncertainty prevails as to where they begin and the company ends, or vice versa.

Winning Through Intimidation

Gonnabees are inherently unsuited by their inability to live in the real world to perform any kind of high-pressure management role. Things usually start to go awry from the moment Gonnabee is named leader. The pampered child takes over and makes terrible, infantile decisions. Then, when these off-the-wall directives create or compound problems, Gonnabee angrily breaks down. His "leadership" style could be labeled "winning through intimidation." He wants to post outstanding results by any means necessary. His subordinates are not people to be led, but pawns to be manipulated. His superficial charm masks an absence of authentic empathy. Other than a craving for admiration, he is totally unconcerned with his followers' feelings. If they "fail him"—or even dare to utter a word of criticism—he fires them without a second thought.

If Gonnabee manages to hang on to his job, it is always at great cost to his colleagues as well as to his own physique. He will suffer from asthma, colitis, migraines, ulcers, alcohol problems, while, of course—for as long as he can—carefully hiding such problems from public view.

Gonnabee's Good-bye

The great irony of the Gonnabee life is that despite the fantastic (a very apt word) drive for success, any actual success never satisfies or lasts. For whenever Gonnabees fall upon good times they continue to suffer pervasive feelings of guilt, unworthiness, and anxiety. Then, unless something or someone is around to save them from themselves, a remorseless mental pressure builds, forever forcing the unconscious to find some way to ease this essentially neurotic discomfort. The dilemma is normally resolved by some kind of unconscious self-sabotage whereby Gonnabee finds some ingenious means of torpedoing his own achievements; which is why so many apparently 'successful' men and women suddenly fall to such apparently mysterious, self-destructive behavior.

Dealing with a Gonnabee

My late colleague Dr. Harry Levinson says that five or so years of classic psychoanalysis can release Gonnabee from his neuroses. The success or failure of this methodology depends upon Gonnabee's willingness to suspend denial for long enough to process and absorb new ideas.

So, yes, lightning can strike. So long as they are not pathological liars—and, be warned, many are— Gonnabee status needs and manipulative skills can be harnessed, usually into sales roles. But they need to be kept on a tight leash. If you acquire a Gonnabee consider making him "president" of a tightly structured marketing division. As long as Gonnabee doesn't have to make important decisions, sales results may be posted. Just never give a Gonnabee a real president's role, for this will assuredly sink the enterprise. If he insists on such promotion, let him go.

Later, when you read or hear of how Gonnabee has become a big success somewhere—maybe even with a close competitor—just reflect that it's Gonnabee whose putting out the puffery and that he's likely riding for a fall. And just rejoice that it won't come at your expense.

These yesteryear thoughts were prescient. Trump had only ever gotten worse. I fell to pondering Jackson's 'gleaming red-light atop the camera' theory of Trump's behavior. Yes of course, Trump is merely a performer. But who lives inside that thespian, a person or a devil? I confess I'm not entirely sure. But maybe our former president could now be helped? It was something to ponder. Meantime, I had signed on with Jackson and Hassan for what, to my chagrin, turned into an interlocking teaching moment. Well, you be the judge...

DOWNSTATE ROLE PLAY

"So great we can share this ride to Downstate." Hassan was happy I'd agreed to attend his prison class. "You've got your driver's license, right?" said Jackson. "As mentioned, we need photo ID to get clearance."

"I'm looking forward to it," I said.

"We recruited fifteen signups for our program," said Hassan. "Twelve identify as African-American, two as Hispanic, and one as Caucasian."

"Only one Caucasian?" I said.

"That's about the norm,"said Jackson.

"And we're the dudes who make the difference," said Hassan.

"We teach what we call communication and personal development. Effectively though, our classes are group therapy,"said Jackson.

"They also get paid a dollar a day for being in the program and get Brownie points for good behavior," said Hassan.

"So, who's there, exactly?"I said.

"Many are doing time for drug-related crimes and several for robbery." Jackson paused. "And some are doing time for murder."

"One guy got shot in a stick-up. Nearly bled to death. Another guy beat up his wife and her lover."

"Ages range from twenty-something to sixty or so. Everyone can read and write but half of them failed to graduate high school. Two are college dropouts and one has a degree with two majors."

"Impressive,"I said.

"One of the bonuses of being in jail is time to study," said Jackson. "He got into that while incarcerated for an earlier crime, then completed outside."

"Most guys like to work out," said Hassan.

"They look tough, and sound tough, and they can seem jaded, but down deep most of them want to learn things—stuff they can apply when they get out,"said Jackson.

"Yeah. For graduates of the class it's a door- opener."

"So, what, exactly, are you teaching?" I said.

"Glad you asked," said Jackson. "Because today we'll need your help." He nodded to Hassan.

"Yeah, we've got a role-play situation for you right here." He plucked a couple of folded pages from his shirt pocket and passed them to me. I looked them over very quickly. "So you want me to play this part?" I asked.

"You got it."

"I think you'll enjoy the whole experience," said Jackson. "And since you're riding in the car with time to kill, I suggest that you read the whole piece right now."

"No problem." I settled back in my seat, and read the role-play.

A Shot at Freedom.

A role play by Jackson Wright and Hassan Just

As chief operating officer for a top corporation, you counseled, coddled, and cajoled a non-performing manager. Nothing seemed to work, so you pointed out that you run a performance-driven business, and that her unit simply wasn't measuring up. She attempted to excuse herself by saying she'd recently fallen pregnant. Then, getting no sympathy for that, she added that her husband had recently been laid-off. Well, life is tough, right? But the scolding did her some good. She seemed to try harder. But not for long. The results didn't show, and a rotten attitude did. So this time you really laid it on the line. No excuses, you said: Have your unit performing by the end of the financial quarter, or be fired. She scuttled home in tears, and complained to her husband that you were subjecting her to emotional abuse. He decided to confront you directly. He called the office a couple of times, but you didn't take the call. So he waited outside your Stamford, Connecticut offices. You emerged just after dusk. He turned out to be an imposing African-American dressed in a pinstripe suit. He was polite enough, but threatening nonetheless. He tried to engage you in conversation but you refused to become involved, and simply walked away. He followed you to your car. It was parked in a lonely yard. Now he was becoming obnoxious. Now you were worried. So, finally, you waved your fist and gave him a piece of your mind. He seemed momentarily stunned. Then a strange look crossed his face and he plunged his hand towards his ominously bulging vest pocket. You'd trained as a marine commando in an earlier career so you immediately sensed that he was reaching for a gun, and your warrior instincts kicked in. You piston-punched him right in the heart. He gasped, crumpled, and fell to the ground. He was immobile, a weird color, and moaning. You bent down and listened closely. He whispered for you to reach into his vest pocket and pull out his bottle of heart pills. You tried to do just that. But it was too late. He lost consciousness and a mere minute or so later was dead. You thought about it for a few moments, then reached for your cell phone and called 911. No less than the local sheriff arrived. With an ambulance wailing unnecessarily in the background, you explained that the irate husband of a disgruntled female employee had accosted you, and then suffered a fatal heart attack. There being no witness, it seemed unnecessary to mention throwing a punch. The whole thing would have faded out, but the widow pressed charges. The incident got a mention in the press and the publicity attracted a passing jogger. She claimed to have witnessed the crucial moment. The district attorney got her to testify that she'd seen you deliver an unprovoked lethal blow. Then he introduced an expert witness to say that the punch, not the heart attack, was the prime cause of death. Your lawyer decided not to put you on the stand. He told the jury that you were a god-fearing Christian, a patriot, and a peace-loving citizen. No punch was ever thrown, he said. The so-called witness was just plain wrong. And, anyway, the entire incident happened after sundown, so nobody could say for sure what happened. He was both confident and persuasive, yet somehow the jury seemed unduly affected by the presence of the grieving and now obviously pregnant widow. Then, as luck would have it, they got instructed by a hard line Hispanic judge with strong feminist leanings. They found you guilty of manslaughter. Finally, in giving sentence, the judge opined that you'd inflicted emotional abuse on an innocent woman, deliberately withheld the truth about the death, and shown absolutely no remorse. That's why, she said, she was sentencing you to five years without parole. Your lawyer said he would appeal, and told you to stick with the story. That was easy. The purported punch was an irrelevant distraction, germane to nothing. You'd never mentioned it to anyone, not your lawyer, who steered you away from so doing, not even your wife—and not a soul since, either. You truly forgot about it. But your appeal was denied. And now you've served three years in this bleak upstate New York prison. But all is not lost. Through the persistent, well-paid machinations of your lawyer, the parole board finally agreed to give you a hearing. If they like what you say they really do have the power to set you free. Your lawyer will be in the room to support you, but the plea itself must come from you alone. You'll have only a few minutes to make your case. Then, depending on how that goes down, they may ask a few questions, at which point your lawyer might be able to fit in a few words, too. Looking through the crack in that door the panel seems like a solemn bunch. The widow is in there too. She wants to see you rot in hell, of course. By the clock on the wall it's ten of a sunless, winter morning. They're all waiting to hear what you have to say. You've given it a lot of thought. So now it's time to get up onto your feet, step out into the room, take a quick look over those expectant faces, and deliver a few well-chosen words…

This was more than I had bargained for. The goal was to choose a message and then, out of those words, in order to persuade a parole board to release a sinner, being in this case, *me*. So whatever should I say to these undoubtedly hard-nosed custodians of the community. I mulled that challenge. It was a clever exercise. And what might Trump do to ace this little test? Even if the parole board refused his plea he would likely win a subsequent battle in the courts.

"I don't see any badges or blue-suited security," I said. Jackson smiled. "And you probably won't. There's only one guard inside this so-called safe area. And most of the time he's likely to be off doing other things. For now there's just us and the inmates. If you get attacked, just shout out. Someone will show up." He straightened up. "So, now, ShowTime." He shot me a smile. "Come meet your judges in the valley of death."

I had no idea of what I might be walking into. But my experience as a priest had taught me something. Helping lost souls can be a challenge. But, right then, attempting to resolve life's core conundrums with denizens of darkness entrapped in a maximum security prison became a rather more mind and stomach churning voyage.

The three of us stepped into an audience of fifteen green-uniformed inmates in a jam-packed 20' x 15' concrete cell. To my surprise everyone seemed delighted to be in the presence of Jackson and Hassan. You really had to be there to catch the warmth of the handshakes and hugs.

Hassan set himself in the chair at the back of the room and Jackson stepped to the battered oak lectern. "Okay you guys," he said, "as you see we have a special guest today. His name is Paul, and as you know he'll be making a plea to the parole board, that being, for the next few hours anyway, as you already know from the advance role-play reading that I distributed last week, none other than your esteemed selves." The guys all smiled. "And so, we call on Paul to make his plea."

I stepped to the lectern. The faces had morphed from happy to stern. They were clearly taking their temporary appointment to Parole Board status seriously. I could not help but wonder why Jackson was so keen—desperate, even— to share his world with a conclave of convicts? Perhaps the universe had planted us all here for a reason? If so, whatever can anyone ever say that hasn't already been said, to transform another person's life?

Looking back, and even at the time, I was struck by how these men in green uniforms took this role-play exercise seriously and embrace their parts as parole board members. Betraying no emotion, they listened to every word I said. And then they asked me exactly the kinds of serious questions that one might have expected from a parole board. Soon enough they plumbed my Trumpian excuses. For me anyway, it all seemed to go haywire.

"Yes, you made a fatal error" said Jackson, on the ride back home into the city.

"Yeah." Hassan broke a smile. "You told the parole board a big lie, and you got found out."

"I should have followed my heart. Instead, I played what I thought would be most persuasive."

"And lied like a Trumpster."

"I figured, in that situation anyway, the Donald might know how to come out a winner."

"Big mistake. These guys know all the angles."

"They know the Trumpian playbook backwards?"

"They know to listen for the truth… in a parole board situation, anyway." Jackson gathered his thoughts then shared them in a stream of consciousness. "In everyday business dealings integrity usually revolves on the matter of honoring one's word. When we say someone is a person of his word, we mean more than that he simply keeps his word. We mean, too, that he understands what he's said, and that he intends to stick to both the word and spirit of the agreement struck, even though doing so might render him, one way or another, out of pocket. We know that he would rather lose his money than his integrity—which he believes would be the certain consequence of failing to keep his word… But in what we call the real world, such sentiments can seem like luxuries, so a lot of people pretend to be exponents of the win-win deal while secretly plotting the downfall of their opponents."

"And in prison too, it's often the only way to go."

"Among themselves, in predicaments where surviving incarceration is on the line, they'll say whatever longevity demands."

"We've got to survive if we want to be free."

"So these guys who graduate your classes are street-smart," I said. Then a question wafted into my head. Maybe I shouldn't have asked it, but I'm glad I did. "Did you ever get jailed yourself?"

Jackson shot me a glance. "No one's above the law, right?… So, *Yes*. I got picked up by the police and carted off to jail. It was quite a learning experience. Right now I'm including that story in a book of what I've learned in prison," said Jackson, taking his eye off the road ahead for just a moment. "If you like, I could PDF you some moments of what Byrne might call evil behavior."

"Sure—I'd love to read up on those," I said.

Jackson made good on his word again. And, again, I got more than I bargained for.

> *In my dream I was standing before Saint Peter at the Pearly Gates. His face was orange but his hands were pale. He slowly shook his head from side to side and waved me away. I tried to speak, but he pointed his finger at my throat and struck me dumb. He reached into his gown, withdrew an AK-47, aimed at me, and prepared to pull the trigger . . .*

COIN OF THE REALM

The digital clock beside my bed was blinking 3:00 AM and the rise and rise of Donald Trump was keeping me awake. His ability to slip a noose had been amazing. We thought the Pussygate saga would end his attempt at the Presidency. But he won the Electoral College and thereby picked up all the marbles. Maybe there's no God? Or maybe the Russians were helping him. What the hell? Then, after Biden beat him in 2020, he refused to leave and stirred his wild insurrection. To be fair, we all excuse ourselves for siding with our feelings. Those blue-collar workers used to make a decent living assembling cars and so on. But then the robots took those jobs. Now those men are unemployed—and angry. Just like too many tawny men had always been. *Cometh the hour, Cometh Trump*—and the whole MAGA movement. That's my take as a psychologist. Yes, yes. I'm a cocktail of psychology and religiosity. But my head rules my heart. Mostly anyway. I turned over and ever so slowly went back to a fitful sleep. When morning finally arrived, I slipped into my gray velvet dressing gown, brewed a coffee, switched on my computer, and penned what I hoped might be a Guest Essay for the *New York Times*. As you might imagine, given everything that had gone down that day, the subject was Donald Trump.

CAN AMERICANS TRUST DONALD TRUMP?

'The coin of the realm for any president is trust.'—Leon Panetta

The bedrock of human development is the formation of capacity to trust. This is typically absorbed by children between six and 18 months. Bear in mind, when Donald Trump was merely five years of age, the mother of a next-door neighbor placed her son in the backyard playpen. After going inside for a few minutes, she returns to find that little Donald had wandered over to the fence that divided the property, and was throwing rocks at her son. So, too, as a delinquent adolescent, Donald Trump trekked into Manhattan to purchase switchblade knives.

He went immediately from college to the Trump management organization, drawing a handsome salary. Effectively, Donald Trump has been institutionalized for most of his adult life, so there is no way to know how he would thrive or even survive on his own in the real world

Donald Trump has boasted of his total lack of trust: "People are too trusting. I'm a very untrusting guy… Hire the best people, and don't trust them… The world is a vicious and brutal place… Even your friends are out to get you: they want your job, your money, your wife."

And bear in mind a key element of his father's leadership style: he always made his subordinates and supplicants come to him, either at his Brooklyn office or at his house in Queens, and he remained seated while they stood.

His zeitgeist is drenched with a sense of danger and his need to project bully-boy toughness. His father trained him to be not just a winner but also a killer. In fact, the father was unable to tame Trump. So, as a punishment, he sent his thirteen year-old son to a down-market military school. But Trump came out of that environment more the bully-boy than ever. In Trump's own words "man is the most vicious of all animals and life is a series of battles ending in victory or defeat."

In the years that Donald Trump has been in our face almost daily, he has sown mistrust in all his Republican rivals, alienated much of the conservative Republican block he needs in the House for legislative success, ignored congressional Democrats, and viciously insulted Democratic leaders, calling them liars, clowns, stupid, and incompetent, condemning Barack Obama as 'sick' and Hillary Clinton as 'the Devil.' When he represents the American people abroad, his belligerent behavior and disrespect for leaders of our closest allies rips apart the comity and peacekeeping pledges built over decades. Yet he never hesitates to congratulate despots, such as Turkey's Erdogan, Egypt's General Sisi, and, most lavishly, Russia's Vladimir Putin.

As President, Trump systematically shredded trust in the institutions he commanded. Having discredited the entire 17-agency intelligence community as acting like Nazis, he also dismissed the judiciary because of one judge's Hispanic background and another's opposition to his travel [the Muslim] ban. Even his Supreme Court justice Neil Gorsuch said it was disheartening and demoralizing to hear Trump disparage the judiciary. Not content to smear the media on a daily basis, Trump borrowed a phrase used by Lenin and Stalin to brand the American media as 'an enemy of the people.'

By his own words, Trump assumed that everyone was out to get him. And paranoia is the tendency toward excessive or irrational suspicion and distrust of others. For a man who proclaims his distrust of everyone, it is not surprising that Trump drew conspiracy theorists closest to him.

A leader who cannot trust subordinates cannot inspire trust. Trump boasts of fierce personal loyalty, he himself is loyal only until he isn't. Where Trump succeeds in inspiring trust is by gifting subordinates the license to lie. In fact, this virus has spread from the White House to congressional Republicans. As the chaos of the White House role plays out, this hide-and-seek commander-in-chief began sending out his most trusted national security advisers to defend him, then cut the legs out from under them. It was never possible for his advisers to know where they stood. His anxious aides must have known how easy it is to fail his loyalty test, and to be the fall guy when a scapegoat was needed.

Lack of trust was even more dangerous on a global scale. Even now, he sees alliances such as NATO as suspect; he sees trade agreements such as NAFTA as ripping off America. This is because Trump's worldview is that we live in the snake pit where everybody is out for themselves. He and his co-conspiracy friends take everything the outsourced white working class hates about globalization, and turn it into personalized enemies: Muslims, Mexicans, and refugees they believe that are taking away their jobs. "Those people are not like us," he says, "they're polluting our blood." Trump creates his extreme manipulation of reality. He insists his subordinates defend his unreality as normal. He then expects the rest of society to accept it, despite the lack of any evidence. This leads to malignant normality; the gradual acceptance by a public inundated with toxic untruths, until his lies pass for normal.

His fundamental goal in life is self-promotion. Yet, what is an extreme narcissistic personality when he wins glorification? How does he dodge humiliation when he is exposed as sacrificing the nation's security on the altar of his infantile need to impress Russian officials by gifting sensitive foreign intelligence? An abyss of self-loathing lies beneath the grandiose behavior of every narcissist. The person Trump trusts least is himself. The humiliation of being widely exposed as a "loser," unable to bully through the actions he promised during the campaign, could drive him to prove that he is, after all, a 'killer.'

I reread the piece. It looked okay. But maybe, before formally submitting it to the Times, an objective look-over would be wise. I attached the file to an email, tapped out a message:

> Hi Byrne: I'm hoping the *New York Times* might publish this attached piece of mine, but before I submit to them, can you be so kind as to cast your eagle eye over it?

WITCH HUNT

Byrne has a knack for showcasing his underlying religious fundamentalism, so his reply did not catch me entirely by surprise . . .

> Hi, Paul, I read the draft of your Op-Ed piece for the *New York Times*. Personally, I might add a couple of paragraphs. First, I would mention the cruelty of Trump's father Fred, which surely exacerbated his son's distrust of authority. Second, you should probably mention DJT's obsession with witch hunts, a phrase he used more than 300 times during his presidency. As it happens, I've fulfilled my promise to share my research into witch hunting. It might be a whole lot more than you need, but here's the attachment, so see what you think.

> Definition

> Early Christian theologians attribute responsibility to the Devil for persecution, heresy, witchcraft, sin, natural disasters, human calamities, and whatever else went wrong. So the state burned heretics and witches. Popular fears, stirred to fever pitch in the 14th and 15th centuries, sustained frenzied efforts to wipe out heretics, witches, and unbelievers, especially Jews. The term 'witch-hunt' can be used as a metaphor for the ostracism of a person or group, often based on their political persuasions.

> Even today, belief in witchcraft and outbreaks of witch-hunts are universal, as too are attempts to use magic to influence personal well-being—to advance a career, win love, increase sexual potency, and so on.

> A Brief History of Witchery

> Punishment for malevolent magic is addressed in the earliest law codes which were preserved, in both ancient Egypt and Babylonia. The Hebrew Bible condemns sorcery. Deuteronomy 18:10–2 states: 'No one shall be

found among you who makes a son or daughter pass through fire, who practices divination, or is a soothsayer, or an augur, or a sorcerer, or one that casts spells, or who consults ghosts or spirits, or who seeks oracles from the dead. For whoever does these things is abhorrent to the Lord'; and Exodus 22:18 prescribes: "thou shalt not suffer a witch to live.'

Perhaps the most notorious witch trial in history was the trial of Joan of Arc. Although the trial was politically motivated, and the verdict later overturned, the position of Joan as a woman and an accused witch became significant factors in her execution. Joan's punishment of being burned alive (victims were usually strangled before burning) was reserved solely for witches and heretics, the implication being that a burned body could not be resurrected on Judgment Day.

Transition to the early modern witch-hunts

The belief in witchcraft, which in the medieval period had been part of the folk religion of the uneducated rural population at best, was incorporated into an increasingly comprehensive theology of Satan. In 1484, Pope Innocent VIII issued a Papal bull authorizing the 'correcting, imprisoning, punishing and chastising' of devil-worshippers who have 'slain infants', among other crimes. Three years later in 1487, Kramer published the notorious *Malleus Maleficarum* (*Hammer against the Evildoers*) which, by virtue of newly invented printing presses, was reprinted in 14 editions by 1520 and became unduly influential in the secular courts.

The witch trials in Early Modern Europe came in waves. The belief in the supernatural now signaled a pact with the Devil. To justify the killings, some Christians of the time and their proxy secular institutions deemed witchcraft as being associated to wild Satanic ritual parties in which there was naked dancing and cannibalistic infanticide. It was also seen as heresy for going against the first of the ten commandments ("You shall have no other gods before me") or as violating majesty, in this case referring to the divine majesty, not the worldly. Further scripture was also frequently cited, especially the Exodus decree that 'thou shalt not suffer a witch to live.'

In England, between 1644 and 1647 'Witchfinder General' Matthew Hopkins charged hefty fees for witch-hunting sprees; stripping his victims naked to find the Witches' mark, then 'pricking' their skin or strapping an imagined witch to a chair and throwing her into a vessel of water to see if she floated.

The 1647 book, *The Discovery of Witches*, soon became an influential legal text. The book was used in the American colonies as early as May 1647, when Margaret Jones was executed for witchcraft in Massachusetts, the first of 17 people executed for witchcraft in the Colonies from 1647 to 1663. The Salem witch trials followed in 1692–1693.

Witchcraft was a normal part of everyday life. Witches were often called for, along with religious ministers, to help the ill or deliver a baby. They held positions of spiritual power in their communities. When something went wrong, no one questioned either the ministers or the power of the witchcraft. Instead, they questioned whether the witch intended to inflict harm or not.

In addition to known witch trials, witch hunts were often conducted by vigilantes, who may or may not have executed their victims. A popular method called "scoring above the breath" meant slashing across a woman's forehead in order to remove the power of her magic. This was seen as a kind of emergency procedure which could be performed in absence of judicial authorities.

Witchcraft or sorcery remains a criminal offense in Saudi Arabia. In November 2009, 118 people were arrested in the province of Makkah that year for practicing magic and 'using the Book of Allah in a derogatory manner,' 74% of them being female. According to Human Rights Watch in 2009, prosecutions for witchcraft and sorcery are proliferating and "Saudi courts are sanctioning a literal witch hunt by the religious police."

• In 2006, an illiterate Saudi woman, Fawza Falih, was convicted of practicing witchcraft, including casting an impotence spell, and sentenced to death by beheading after allegedly being beaten and forced to finger-point.

• In 2007, Mustafa Ibrahim, an Egyptian national, was executed, having been convicted of using sorcery in an attempt to separate a married couple.

• On 12 December 2011, Amina Abdulhalim Nassar was beheaded in Al Jawf Province after being convicted of practicing witchcraft and sorcery. So, too, Muree bin Ali bin Issa al-Asiri was beheaded on 19 June 2012 .

The situation might be even worse in Africa. In March 2009, Amnesty International reported that up to 1,000 people in the Gambia had been abducted by government-sponsored 'witch doctors' on charges of witchcraft, and taken to detention centers where they were forced to drink poisonous concoctions.

Byrne was right of course. It was infinitely more than I needed to know about witchery. I was thinking about responding to him, when another email arrived, this time from Jackson, whose take on the evil all around us, to which we're mostly oblivious, was, for me anyway, a spellbinder...

THE TOMBS

Hi there Paul. I'm attaching the piece on my arrest in the era of Manhattan's Giuliani. On 9/11 (2001) he proclaimed himself America's Mayor—and most everyone agreed. These days everyone sees him for the evil toad he always was. Time wounds all heels.

Margot and I were journeying home after seeing *The Judas Kiss*, the Broadway play that emanated from Oscar Wilde's tragic fall into the hell of a Victorian prison. The New York crowd was pressing as we entered the subway. Margot, her 'smart' Metro card in hand, peered over my shoulder. The turnstile bar abruptly opened, hurtling us into the underground. Margot, not grasping what had happened, was drawn onto the escalator and was gone. "That woman with you didn't pay!" shouted a bellicose officer. "*You're* under arrest! Where's your ID?" Alas, I possessed only my Metro card theater program and a $5 bill.

I was cuffed, traipsed into the Broadway lights, and vigorously frisked. I attracted odd, embarrassed looks from the subway hordes. Perhaps they'd not previously seen a handcuffed, bespectacled, silver-headed, fifty-eight-year-old in neat khaki trousers and jacket, blue shirt, and tie, restrained within the phalanx of gun-toting cops.

I reflected that British Officialdom paraded Oscar Wilde in handcuffs and leg irons at Reading Station. Poor Oscar broke down and wept. I'm a little more sanguine. I was in my third year of running a class at Rikers Island, teaching inmates—quite a few of whom were incarcerated for armed robbery—how to make their way in the 'real world.' I figured I wouldn't meet anyone more sinister in the downtown cell.

I was taken to the Midtown booking station, relieved of my shoelaces, belt, and tie, then photographed, fingerprinted, and tossed into a dark holding cell. "How's your evening been?" I inquired of a gray-haired cellmate. "Ah'm Dwayne and ah'm homeless," he responded. "Ah hope to be out in time to hustle breakfast." A couple of ladies-of-the-night on the other side of the wire grating paid no attention.

I phoned Margot. She was distraught. She'd boarded the waiting downtown N train—assuming I was on it too—and alighted to a scene from *The Vanishing*.

Shortly after midnight, Dwayne and I and two other venerable citizens, cuffed behind our backs, crammed into the back row of a customized minibus. Seven police officers filled the front three rows. The driver, apparently a frustrated Grand Prix driver, careened the vehicle across Manhattan toward the West Side Highway. I was transfixed by the sight of the needle pushing 50-plus miles per hour. Other than to hit the accelerator and sound a burst on the siren at the red lights on the avenues, this daredevil was oblivious to others on the road. It was a chase scene from a bad movie. Dwayne's eyes were popping. We both knew that without control over our hands or bodies, we'd be hard-pressed to survive if this thrill-seeker rolled the vehicle.

The twisting tarmac rushed to the windscreen. Dwayne's fragile frame jammed into the left side of my rib cage, and my right ear crested onto the side window as we swung onto the highway. Our pilot revved the volume on a tape of boom-boom salsa and jammed his foot to the floor. Assorted officers sounded a gleeful cacophony of foul language as we vanquished all comers on the race downtown.

But we lived. At around 1:00 A.M. we clambered down a dingy iron stairwell into the 'Tombs,' the infamous underground maze that imprisons persons convicted of no offense awaiting the first hearing. The guards were a mixture. Some were keen enough to help, but many were as surly as trained circus animals, performing but resenting it. Several had given up all pretense to civility and were mindlessly churlish and autocratic. One wouldn't want to let these fellows off the leash.

My cuffs were removed, and I got back my tie, belt, and shoelaces. The Tombs came as a surprise: invasive fluorescent lights, freshly painted hospital-green walls and bars, freshly disinfected, sparkling gray concrete floors. I shared a cell with 18 inmates. Half a dozen had commandeered the 2-foot-wide stainless-steel bench that snaked the cell perimeter. The rest sought repose upon the floor. A gleaming stainless-steel toilet bowl occupied the corner. A pay phone jutted from the wall. Dwayne pressed a quarter into my hand. I told Margot I'd be okay.

My mind raced. Who'd dare take issue with our mayor's potent crime-crushing policies? Rudy Giuliani was a classic rule-by-fear and show-quick-results leader. He might never approve of the hair-raising race to the Tombs – yet in a way he already did, for his minions knew what they could get away with. They knew he'd look the other way if anyone complained. But no matter, for where's the harm in the inadvertent incarceration of an apparent turnstile-beater—or anyone without proper ID, for that matter—so long as the city was made safe for decent people? I insinuated myself under the steel bench, fashioned my jacket into a pillow, and sought answers.

4:00 A.M. and breakfast: cornflakes, milk, and an apple. I surveyed the diners. Half were in for quality-of-life crimes: smoking weed, urinating behind a tree in a public carpark, drivers-license anomalies, jumping turnstiles. Dwayne's crime was vagrancy. Four were would-be armed robbers. One proudly displayed an old world war wound, a wicked shot in the back. "I'll be on the island," he said. "How do I qualify for your class?" Dwayne got an early call. I produced my $5 bill. "Here's breakfast, Dwayne."

At 3:00 P.M. I was called upstairs into a grungy, steel-doored confessional. "I suggest you accept an immediate conditional dismissal," said an assigned legal-aid defender. "You could fight and sue the city, but you'd be looking at investing time and money."

"Sue the city?" I said. "I live here. So do my wife and kids. My friends, too. I *am* the city."

A dozen inmates on my side of the grate paced the floor. Carl, now 41, had been in and out of prison since age 18. His front teeth were missing; he was overweight and without marketable skills. Yet he was a nice guy–intelligent too. He declined the offer of community service. "I'd be working without pay. I'd never support myself. I'm better off at Rikers." Kevin, a feisty Irish youth with a black eye, complained that this time his father had refused to hire a private lawyer to get him off. "What kind of father does this to his son?" he wailed.

A 31 year-old construction worker said that when his wife got pregnant he couldn't afford to pay the parking fine, so his license got suspended. No problem, so long as she drove the car. But when the time came to drive her to the hospital, he took the wheel. He got pulled over on a DWB, Driving While Black. Now he'd lost a day's work–$120. I told him my story, and his face lit up. "Hey! Now you know how the police treat *us*!"

"Every day of our lives," chimed a winsome West Indian. "You gotta tell them."

"Yes, people don't believe us, but they'll believe *you*."

All this innocent faith in my powers was touching and depressing.

I accepted the judge's dismissal–and suddenly

realized what was wrong. In Giuliani's Manhattan the cop preempted justice; proportionality was a lost value—virtually any perceived offense may carry automatic arrest and incarceration. That was quite a penalty. What judge would jail anyone for $1.50? But the Red Queen's rules applied: punishment first, injustice later. The cost of a private lawyer to fight a wrongful arrest cost at least $1,000 and a day off work. For some, like me, it didn't matter much. I could afford a legal bill, and the day off work was enlightening. But others less fortunate were sorely punished. The arrest record was capriciously swollen, and our big brother world could be unforgiving—legally, financially, and emotionally. A wronged person feels impotent, bitter, and alienated. Autocracy is a very effective sword. But it has two edges. Giuliani was wielding it to show astonishing results, but they came at a price, just the same. His successor would inherit more problems than anyone realized.

Margot and I strolled out into a sunny late-spring afternoon. Trees were verdant, and birds were singing. I was relieved, exultant even. Freedom—never take it for granted. I stopped stock still. "We're walking atop the tombs," I explained. "The prisoners are beneath our feet, literally." Indeed. A hapless mass of quality-of-life offenders, the wretched refuse of a gleaming city, our truly needy, our tired and poor, incarcerated but not yet convicted, neatly packed together within sturdy iron bars set into shimmering, freshly disinfected concrete floors, were huddled, hurting, and yearning to breathe free, right then in there.

So what did I learn? I learned to shy from an unforgiving system. I learned to be wary of the police in my own backyard. I learned to love a homeless man. I learned to seize the best in whatever comes my way.

I paused to ponder Jackson's descent into the Tombs. Angels and devils seemed to be down there. If so, then, as Byrne likes to say, they're all around us. For sure, evil is as evil does. I resumed reading...

> Two days later I was back on Rikers Island for my regular class for inmate denizens. There's a highly effective prison grapevine so the entire class knew of my arrest and I was something of a hero. I opened my class with a droll joke. "Fellow inmates," I said to laughter and applause. I then explained that getting handcuffed and spending the night in the Tombs had given me greater insight into their own predicaments. In recalling the experience, however, I began to relive it. I felt a rush of shame and anger. I choked back a lump in my throat and did my best to hide the welling of tears in my eyes. The class immediately sensed that I'd been more shaken up by my incarceration than I'd quite realized. Empathizing with my unresolved feelings and incipient tears, they very compassionately permitted me to gather myself and move to the day's lesson on the everlasting lesions of racism.
>
> The moral, I suppose is that my prison classes taught me that most lost souls are intelligent, caring, decent human beings whose antisocial tendencies mostly spring from battered upbringings. They're skilled outlaws but impotent citizens. Their salvation—and mine and everyone else's—likely rests within the lessons that incarceration can teach.

My gaze fell back to Jackson's email postscript...

> There it is, Paul. Quite a learning experience, right?
> Just saying...
> Jackson

Yes. Or, as Byrne might say, it was an education in good and evil. Or, as the psychologist within me prefers, between good and bad behavior. Which in turn propelled me forward...

BESTIAL DEEDS

Hoping to inject some psychological rationality into Byrne's fiction of witches and devils, I invested a few hours of my time, created a PDF, and attached it to my response to him. You may be the best judge of whether I was out of line...

> Well, yes, Byrne. Thanks for the insight on witch-hunts. It's tragic, I think, that I know next to nothing about evil. As we all know, in modern times, a baptized Roman Catholic, Adolf Schickelgruber, as I recall, made it lawful to cast out Jews, torture them, send them to gas chambers, murder them en masse, then bury them in unmarked graves. So, I'm attaching my take on the psychology of heinous behavior...

It is not easy to seriously discuss bestial acts of human against human that challenge our basic conception that human nature is good. But my psychological training has taught me to reject the Christian notion of a devil as some form of inner Lucifer. I do accept, however, the need to analyze the upbringing of individuals who engage in bestial behavior, such as Hitler, Stalin, Idi Amin, and Pol Pot.

So, what is the line one crosses to go from being a good dutiful citizen to a mass murderer with no conscience for the bestial deeds and no remorse for destroying human lives? And how is this furrow maintained? What would it take for you or me to slide across it? It seems to me that you want to believe that this line is with us here forever and with them over there permanently. In fact we, the good ones, could all too quickly become them, the bad ones. Let me give you an example:

Imagine a traitor is sentenced to death by firing squad and the government wants to recruit his peers, civilians, to shoot him. Few volunteer. If, however, they add a condition that only one of six guns will have a real bullet in the chamber, thus each gun would have only a small likelihood of being the lethal weapon, typically more volunteer. Why? Employing the tactic of diffusion of responsibility greases that line, and some good people are ready to slide across the boundary, become killers for the state.

The Milgram Experiments

Stanley Milgram—just in his twenties at the time—created a series of experiments to plumb the apparent mystery of why they went down that route—and whether right here in America, our citizens might sometime do the same.

His Jewish heritage contributed to him seeking an answer to the question: "If Hitler asked you, would you execute a stranger?" As I'm sure you know, Milgram recruited more than 1,000 participants from all walks of life. They arrived individually in the lab and were told they were helping science find new ways that punishment might improve memory and thereby the process of education.

Teacher, the role assigned to the participant, helps the Experimenter, who is wearing the white lab coat, symbolic of his status, to connect the Learner, a lovable middle-aged man, to the electrical shock apparatus; the victim is in an adjacent room. On the first trials, learning is going well. But then the Learner starts making errors and punishment begins, first small, then ever escalating.

'Who will be responsible if something bad happens in there to the Learner, Sir?' asks the Teacher. "I will; please continue, Teacher." At 375 volts, the Learner screams, there is a loud thud, and then only silence from the shock chamber thereafter. But the experiment is not yet over. There are five more higher levels possible to the extreme of 450 volts.

What I personally find amazing is that before starting

his research, Milgram invited 40 psychiatrists to predict the percentage and type of person who would indeed go all the way in this study that he described to them in detail. In their collective wisdom based on their medical training in dispositional, individualistic analysis, they concluded that fewer than 1% of the Teacher-Participants would go all the way, and they would be the sadists. But the psychiatrists were all wrong. Two thirds of all the subjects went all the way up to the final level. So, by exploiting our deeply ingrained learned behavioral patterns of obedience, ordinary citizens can be seduced into behaviors that lead to killing innocent victims.

Zimbardo and the Stanford Prison Experiment

Or consider the work of Zimbardo. A contemporary of Milgram, he conducted the Stanford Prison Experiment. Effectively, he 'incarcerated' good students in a mock prison where they descended into violence, and became torturers.

A colleague extended the basic paradigm by manipulating the actors' perception of their victims. A group of college students expected to help train another group of students from a nearby college by collectively shocking them when they erred on the task. Just as the study was about to begin, the participants overheard the assistant tell the experimenter one of three phrases:

- Neutral: 'The subjects from the other school are here.'

- Humanized: 'The subjects from the other school are here; they seem "nice."'

- Dehumanized: 'The subjects from the other school are here, they seem like "animals."'

They never saw those other students, or heard anything directly from them; this was the only label that they had to go on. The boys who imagined their victims as 'animals' progressively elevated their shock levels over each trial after the first, significantly more than the neutral control.

So a one-word label can create a stereotype of the victim, of the enemy, that also lowers the height of that line between good and evil and enables more good people to cross over and become perpetrators.

The validity of this construct has been demonstrated by the lynching and burning alive of untold numbers of Black men in the U.S., usually based on fears of their sexual conquest of White women, facilitated by the dehumanizing label of "nigger."

They never saw those other students, or heard anything directly from them; this was the only label that they had to go on. The boys, who imagined their victims as 'animals,' progressively elevated their shock levels over each trial after the first, significantly more than the neutral control.

So a one-word label can create a stereotype of the victim, of the enemy, that also lowers the height of that line between good and evil and enables more good people to cross over and become perpetrators.

All of which brings us to the so-called *Lucifer Effect*: humans cannot be defined as good or evil—what we do depends upon the situation. One way or another, 'good' people can be persuaded to perform 'evil' behavior.

I couldn't help but wonder what Jackson would make of all this, so when his reply came in, and it came in fairly quickly actually, I was intrigued. As I think you will be too.

THE POWER GAME

Thanks for including me, Paul, in your emailed profile of Trump. And to you Byrne, in your take on the historical popularity of witch hunting—and perhaps devil worshiping— and why these all-too-human inclinations are still with us today. What I think you guys might be missing is that Trump is fully engaged in what I call the Power Game.

THE POWER GAME

The Power Game is akin to chess. A group of courtiers forms around the king. On his own, he's pretty weak, so he needs the other pieces to survive. And they need to protect him, or they're out of the game. But unlike chess pieces, people have ideas and feelings. So imagine a game of chess where all your chessmen had passions, intellects, and dollops of cunning. You'd be uncertain of your opponent's pieces and your own, too. What if your knight could shuffle himself onto a new square on the sly? What if your bishop, in disgust at your castling, could wheedle your pawns out of their places? And what if your pawns, hating you because they are pawns, could sneak away from the protective positions you'd assigned them purely for the pleasure of seeing you checkmated. You might be the smartest person in the world, yet still be beaten by your own pawns. Most people pursue power decently. In fact we have to be congenial and cunning. Everything has to appear decent and democratic, but if the players adhere too rigidly to the rules they get hammered by those who don't. The best way to win is to choose words very carefully and excel at the game. Language exerts hidden power. It's the quick way to become a better friend, lover, and provider. If we make others feel good about themselves, they'll always want to be around us. The simple fact is that if the power game is unavoidable, then it's better to be deft than

dopey. Nothing about power is natural. It's neither moral
nor immoral, and it's not good or evil, either. It's a game.
So stay calm and play to win. But it's pointless to attain a
worthy goal at a ruinous price, so never get dragged into
a losing situation.

Ah, yes. Jackson was ever the pragmatist. I suspected this piece
might spark Byrne into even more research. So I was not at
all surprised to receive this next follow-up missive from my
dear, and, it seemed, increasingly fundamentalist friend. See
what you think…

LYING DEVILS

Hi there, Paul and Jackson. In thinking about everything that you guys raised, I got to thinking about a book I read a while ago, *The People of the Lie* by M. Scott Peck, a Christian and psychiatrist who says Christianity has valid insight into human evil. I'm attaching what I gleaned from a quick reread of his insights...

Evil is cloaked in normality so it mostly goes unnoticed. But its everyday banality is dangerous. The self-interest of evil-doers trumps (pun intended) truth and social welfare. So they exploit others for personal gain or satisfaction, and a veneer of respectability makes them particularly insidious and destructive.

They're skilled at identifying and exploiting vulnerabilities, and fabricating elaborate falsehoods. Lying is both a cause and manifestation of their evil nature. They're masters of disguise. Any goodness is a level of pretense. They're can't admit to flaws, and deny the harm they inflict. They use scapegoats to divert attention from their shortcomings. Their denials are supported by the defense mechanism of projection: they routinely and unconsciously ascribe their undesirable qualities to others. They're typically charming, so their dance of self-deception is not always visible. Their façade of normalcy or even virtue can be convincing. They can do all this for long periods, leaving emotional and psychological wreckage in their wake.

The evil in this world is committed by self-righteous, spiritual fat cats, the Pharisees of our own day. A sense of personal sin is the only effective safeguard against our own proclivity for evil. But evil people shy from the light of psychotherapy. Instead, they don masks of piety, and infiltrate our churches, maybe even as deacons or dignitaries.

Sure, much that can be blamed on the demonic can be explained by traditional psychiatric dynamics. But we need to take the demonic realm seriously. You may scoff at the idea of possession, but evil is more than psychological dysfunction. It is a spiritual malaise that affects the core of human existence.

So here's my conclusion… We automatically assume this is a naturally good world that has somehow been contaminated by evil. In terms of science, however, evil accords with the natural law of physics. That children generally lie and steal and cheat is routinely observable. The fact that they mostly grow up to become honest adults seems more remarkable. It might even make more sense to assume this is a naturally evil world that has somehow mysteriously been 'contaminated' by goodness than the other way around.

But the Bible tells us that God made a good world, and then it fell into sin. And God has a plan. We await the Second Coming and the Final Redemption. Then we will have a good world once again. Meantime we sense in our hearts that something has gone wrong in this world and we long for Eden. There is a place for psychiatry and psychotherapy, but we need it within a biblical view of this world, as that is where our ultimate hope and healing is to be found. As Jesus said in Mark 2:17, "It is not the healthy who need a doctor, but the sick. I have not come to call the righteous, but sinners."

And here's yet another email from Jackson. And this one looks like bad news...

BACK TO THE FUTURE

Jackson is level-headed so I took his concern seriously...

Hi there again, you guys!

The *New York Times* has a piece about a guy named Russ Vought and a bunch of Trumpsters who have created what they are calling Project 2025.

Seems Vought—a Trump former budget chief and a self-described Christian nationalist—is crafting proposals for Trump to deploy the military to quash civil unrest, seize more control over the Justice Department, and assert the power to withhold congressional appropriations—and that's just on Trump's first day back in office. Seems he'll steer this agenda from an influential White House perch, potentially as Trump's chief of staff. He says 'the left has corrupted the nation's laws and institutions.' He aims to stock federal agencies with disciples to wage wars on abortion and immigration.

Trump blessed Vought's agenda at a Mar-a-Lago fundraiser. He says conservatives need to overpower the bureaucracy and centralize authority in the Oval Office. It's a kind of Anglo-Protestant cultural supremacism. His allies are racial and religious supremacists. They plan to gut the FBI and give the president more oversight over the Justice Department. They say they're going to rip and shred the federal government apart, and if you don't like it, you can lump it.

Just saying / Jackson

Yes indeed, that this plan had only just come to light was truly worrying. On the bright side, the best laid plans of mice and men often go astray, and the Trumpsters would surely lose the November election. Or, before those dice are cast, he might well wind up serving time in prison. Just as I was mulling these happy thoughts my phone vibrated. And I didn't need to pull it to my ear to catch the distress...

LOOSE CANNON

"Can anyone believe it?" Byrne's voice was loaded with anxious incredulity. "This out-of-her-depth Federal Judge, and out and out Trumpster, Aileen Cannon, has just given Trump a *Get Out Of Jail Free* card... She's reached way above her pay-grade and formally ruled that *any* appointment of *any* Special Counsel is unconstitutional."

"She fired Jack Smith?"

"Indeed she did."

"Wow!"

"His case against Trump for stealing secret documents from the White House was open and shut."

"It was the strongest of all the indictments."

"It was ironclad."

"There'll be an appeal, surely."

"And a delay. Trump's lawyers will string it out until after the election."

"Of course. Trump is desperate to stay out of jail."

"She knows exactly what she's doing. She's working with the Devil. She bade Satan into her chambers. He never goes anywhere uninvited."

"Bad behavior is all around us."

"Oh, Paul... I know I'm sounding like a broken record. But you still don't get it. The forces of evil are real. And Aileen Cannon really is a witch."

That night I dreamed of Trump. His image appeared on a television screen on a stage in front of a scarlet curtain. He was sitting behind a boardroom table, wearing a red cape and holding a fiery three-pronged fork. He seemed to be speaking in tongues and mocking an open casket. I jumped onto the stage and stepped behind the curtain. He was sitting on

a golden toilet. As he saw me, his hair morphed into
a starry wizard's cap. He opened his mouth and I
caught the smell of his breath. It was foul and hot.

I shared my nightmare with Byrne. I could have guessed what he'd say. But he took his time. "It's plain as day," he said. "Your unconscious has tapped into the universe. The heavens are warning that we're in a nightmarish situation. I don't say it lightly, but your dream is shouting it at you. Trump really has become possessed by the Devil. Unless we find a way stop him, he'll fulfill Satan's plan." He paused. "Talking to him will achieve nothing. His inner Devil will just play us along. We must arrange an exorcism. It truly is the only way out."

I took a deep breath. I'd left the church because I finally couldn't stomach the smells and the bells and the mumbo-jumbo. So the words that fell from my lips took me by surprise. "Maybe you're right... But if an exorcism truly is the only option, how might we arrange it?"

"I have a friend who might help."

SUPREME TOADIES

Jackson's voice was calm but his message was disturbing.

"The Supremes just dropped their bomb."

"They dropped a bomb? It was always coming," I said.

"They've pulled off the guardrails."

"He's never in his life had any."

"They've declared the Donald a King. He can do whatever he wants now."

"What was the split?"

"Six to three." He paused. "Four to three, actually, since neither Alito nor Thomas recused themselves."

"Amy Coney Barrett could have swung the verdict, but in real life she truly is a Roman Catholic handmaiden."

"So the verdict is beyond redemption?"

"It was just another payoff. Top lawyers and judges—including federal judges and bigwig academics—agree on that. Only toadies are defending the Supremes."

"Byrne says Satan's backing Trump."

"The Donald has his followers, that's for sure."

"One way or another, they've delayed any possibility of a trial for the January sixth insurrection."

"It's not right. It's a travesty. So if you'll excuse me, I may need get myself a cognac."

So the Supremes drove Jackson to drink. But maybe Byrne was right. Maybe those black-robed devils hoped to secure a place in history by lifting their legs and leaving a stain in the sands of time. The founding fathers deliberately created a Constitution to oust imperialists. But now we have an emperor. But look on the bright side. The reign of Ozymandias did not last, and certainly not for as long as he envisioned. And, anyway, come September, our contemporaneous Gonnabees may be headed for the guillotine. As we shall soon enough see.

A STORMY HUSH

"Oh, No. No, no, no." As you might guess, the plaintive voice on my phone belonged to Byrne. "*Another* slow-walk!"

"Huh?"

"Judge Juan Merchan just postponed the New York Hush-Money sentencing."

"Really?"

"Yes. All the way until September the eighteenth."

"Maybe it's good news. Maybe he's done that to get his ducks in a row and preempt any fallout from the Scotus ruling."

"Maybe."

"And he seems a hard-nosed Judge. Come that day, I'm sure he'll do the right thing. Meantime though, I guess our new Emperor will go on living a regal life."

"Oh Paul! Don't you see it? Don't you get it at all? That's exactly the reward of a pact with the Devil. It happened to the Supremes, too. Lucifer *always* looks after his own"

PRISON GRADUATION

I was flattered when Jackson invited me to join him and Margot and Hassan in their sojourn to the Rikers Island graduation of their prison classes. We packed into Jackson's green Mini Minor. Given the heft of Hassan, Jackson assigned him the front passenger seat. I was in the back with Margot, who wore a simple blue suit and matching low heels. The men wore beige jackets and chinos. All of us were excited. So our chattering was pretty well continual.

"So how did you guys come to get this gig?" I asked.

"That's quite a question."

"Yeah. Gotta come up with an answer."

"Margot and I—and then Ashleigh—first got together at another Rikers graduation class. It was something of an out of body experience."

"Margot and I were waiting for our errant son, actually—"

"—he got arrested on account of his drug habit," said Margot.

"And there he was—"

"—a rare white fellow within a sea of amber legs, arms, and faces. An ivy league psychology graduate—"

"But right at home, within a line of felons."

I didn't ask the question of how Jackson and Margot felt about that, but I didn't need to either.

"After the ceremony, the program director introduced herself, and said she'd read that I coached top executives—"

"—and had written a couple of self-help books and was an experienced public speaker."

"So might I be up for teaching a communications and public speaking class?" I asked.

"We're a charity with no money," she said, "so you'd be working gratis as an unpaid volunteer."

"Yeah. So karma was calling," said Hassan

"And that's how, ever since, Jackson and I wound up with only half an income."

We arrived at the Rikers gymnasium with just a few minutes to spare. Ashleigh was there already. She said she'd set it all up. She waved her hand over the space. A three-tiered horseshoe of empty chairs facing a podium and a microphone on the far side of the room. The officials, dignitaries, and family members had informally gathered adjacently, in a conversation circle, with seating scattered around the edges. Most everyone was standing within that sphere, engaged in polite conversation.

I wound up sitting between Ashleigh and Hassan on the side of the third row. Margot and Jackson were alongside us.

Then a portal opened at the side of the gym, and to the soft sighs of family and friends, the graduates, wearing spotless-clean, neatly pressed greens and their best sneakers, entered, and, shooting self-conscious smiles to loved ones, filed to the two front rows seats.

Ashleigh was buoyant. The family members and guests had no idea of what to expect. The guys were smiling, delighted to be sharing the moment, and doubtless imagining that even if Jackson didn't do them proud, he'd at least not bungle, in the presence of their loved ones, this celebratory milestone in their lives—in everyone's life, including my own.

A dour and dumpy nun in a green-trimmed, white half-habit and clutching a black bible, stepped up to deliver a benediction. So much for the separation of church and state. She planted her venerable, newly shined, rubber-soled shoes into the floorboards. In what seemed to me like slow-motion, she levitated her arms. In that moment her voice became commanding, spellbinding even. "Let us rise in prayer," she said. And what happened next was astonishing. She seemed to morph into a floating seraph, and, as if the ceiling had opened, the air seemed lighter and brighter, and every graduate seemed taller and straighter, Godlike almost. Everyone else—teachers, administrators, parents, lovers, and family—seemed supporting players in the climactic moment of a sacred ritual. As best I recall, in seraph tones that seemed to resonate from the walls, she said, "Heavenly Father, we celebrate the enlightenment of men behind prison bars whose crimes deprived them of their freedoms. You alone have brought these men to repentance and a saving faith. They have come to an understanding that in Christ they will be forgiven. And so we pray that you will now send them into the world, to tell of Christ and the forgiveness of sins that comes from Him alone. In Jesus name we pray, Amen."

Did we all share a religious moment? I glanced around. For sure, something unusual had happened. Until I can think of a better explanation, I'm categorizing the experience as something that happened inside my own mind. Or a phenomenon of quantum physics. But I might be wrong. Well, as the kids say these days, Whatever.

Jackson took a deep breath and headed for the lectern. Happily, all the speeches were recorded and Ashleigh sent me the transcripts. Here's what Jackson had to say...

JACKSON SHARES 3 SUBWAY TOKENS

I'm told that when you get out of here, you'll each receive fifty dollars and three subway tokens. That might not sound like all the help you need, but if you think about it right, each of these doubloons is a gem, and as a threesome they're a veritable treasure.

This one, *U.S.A.* (pretends to read those three letters from an inscription on the coin) stands for *Unconditional Self-Acceptance.* It is the healing token of the *heart.* It repeats the simple truth that your inner child is as perfect as the day you were born and that you are as worthy of living a good life as any person on this planet. It reminds you to keep on giving yourself that gift of USA, and to approach the world with confidence and courage.

This one, *Liberty*, is the currency of the *mind*. It reinforces a set of liberating beliefs that begins with your vision of a better life, and proceeds with an attitude of gratitude for your new set of can-do beliefs. Hold this coin and close your eyes and you'll hear yourself say, "Yes indeed, I already possess everything I need, so I truly can achieve the life I want by tapping into my natural talents and gifts."

This one, *SAM*, stands for *Self Affirming Maneuvers* and is the currency of *action*. It reminds you that every word you speak or thing you do, every step, no matter how apparently ordinary, should advance your mission in life. It reminds you to act as if it were impossible to fail—to fake it until you make it.

So there they are… three priceless tokens of USA, Liberty, and SAM. I'm tucking mine back right here next to my heart. You'll get yours at the front gate at 5.00 a.m. on the day of your release. Invest them wisely and good things will follow.

That went down well. Then Hassan stepped up to the plate…

HASSAN RIKERS GUEST SPEECH

First up, I want you guys to put your hands together and thank everyone who put this program together and persevered to help us arrive here today… I didn't know what I was getting into, but whatever it was, I got more of it than I bargained for. I'm honored to be here today. But I'm still something of a rebel, so I'm sure it'll be okay for me to present a poem…

I was bitter, angry and headstrong
But what was wrong?
I prayed, then came a high command:
Your destiny lies in your hands, it said.
Suddenly what all came clear
was the cost of failing to face my fear.
Now, getting wise
I saw the ignorance in arrogance
and tore off its disguise,
Surprise!
I popped the spell of the living hell
I'd known so well.
Now, humbled, I stand and gaze
giving thanks and earnest praise
You set me up in this new phase
where dreams are not impossible to reach
so long as we take care
to practice what we preach.

I've just gotta repeat something I said at my own prison graduation…

> I'm not making no promises to anyone, and you guys shouldn't either… So don't you go promising that when you get out of here you are going to change your life and become a great guy. Don't you make that promise to your father, or your mother, or your brothers or your sisters, or your girlfriend, or your kids. *No! Never!* Listen to me now… we're gonna make that promise *ourselves,* right here and right now—*right?*

SATAN'S SIGNATURE

As I entered his room, Byrne looked up from his iPad. "I'm guessing you never read this piece in the Guardian... *In the heat of the assassination attempt, the bloodied ex-president's defiance created a picture that echoes murals of frontier heroism and religious resurrection. Might that be a warning of what's to come?*" He sighed. "This shooting's a heartbreaker, right?"

"Just one photo may win him a new presidency."

"Social media is saying it was faked."

"Give me a break. Everyone saw that a whizzing bullet drew blood from close to his cunning mind."

"And, like Christ, he rose again."

"With black-clad, sun-glassed Secret Service agents enfolding him. And, in a rerun of his 2016 inauguration speech, he raised his fist and shouted, 'Fight, fight, fight.'"

"But against whom and for what?"

"He's gulling his cultists into thinking that these might be his very last words. He was calling on his so-called patriots to fight in his name, over his bleeding hulk."

"He stayed calm enough to ask for his shoes."

"The bit I don't quite understand is why he told the people trying to get him to safety, to wait while he stuck his head and fist back into the line of fire." I paused. "To be fair, only a conspiracy theorist might try to decipher Donald's paw."

Byrne raised his hands to his temples. "What I think, Paul, is that Trump's habit of fashioning memes with other meanings is Satan's signature."

"Like this failed assassination?"

"Yes."

I thought about that. "Maybe you have a point," I said. "If so, then apparently divinely spared, he rises, bloodied but undaunted, beneath the Stars and Stripes, and reaching for the heavens, from inside a cosset of security agents."

"Blood is thicker than politics or patriotism."

"So evangelicals saw the hand of God in his survival?"

"They saw Christ rising from his tomb."

"Our man became the shining vision of a sacred twenty-first century resurrection."

"The Devil looks after his own." Eyeing me all the while, Byrne took a long pause. "Oh, Paul—you *still* don't get it! Don't you see? At the very beginning of all of this, Trump made a Faustian bargain. The bullet only grazed his ear because Lucifer was protecting him."

"If so, it's ongoing. In the minds of his cultists, a saintly leader raised a rebellious fist in what evangelicals see as God using a born-again sinner to symbolize an erstwhile martyr."

"So the image will win him another presidency?"

"A campaign that begins with bullets, blood, and death is surely an omen of carnage to come."

"Or healing?"

"I heard that Reverend Franklin Graham will attend the Republican National Convention, so he might already have arranged that with the Almighty."

"Oh, happy day?"

"We shall see what we shall see."

Had he been there, and I'm not sure he wasn't, Elmer Gantry would have loved that whole revival circus.

A REVIVAL TRIUMPH

It proved impossible for us to attend the three-day Republican National Convention in Milwaukee. So we—Jackson, Byrne and I—agreed to watch the whole thing on television, then, after the final session, link our iPhones for a discussion. Here's how our conversation went down.

"If we accept that Trump is merely an actor, then, following the storyline of a supernatural intervention"—Byrne's voice was tinged with irony—"the Devil made his entrance as a softer, gentler, spiritually enhanced, candy-peddling grandpa figure, with a white bandage covering his red badge of courage," said Byrne.

"A kiss-me-goodnight father," said Jackson.

"A comforting, avuncular, patriotic healer," said Byrne.

"Franklin Graham's introduction was pretty amazing."

"The *Reverend* Franklin Graham," said Byrne.

"His Christianity was on full display. No inclusion of any other religion. He was there to preach the fiction that the Donald is a man of his word who will make America great again," said Jackson.

"Then came his formal blessing."

"I have to agree with Byrne that the so-called Reverend did a devilish job of that," I said.

"The Donald's opening line, 'I'm not supposed to be here tonight' played into that benediction."

"Perhaps the only time he's told the truth in years," said Byrne.

"He's supposed to be in jail," said Jackson.

"And then, of course, he milked the line: 'I stand before you in this arena only by the grace of Almighty God Bullets were flying over us, yet I felt serene... 'I felt very safe because I had God on my side..."

"Marjorie Taylor Greene said she saw an angel."

"She confused an angel with a sniper."

"Don Junior said his father faced danger with the heart of a lion."

"Some other worshipper declared that the Devil came to Pennsylvania holding a rifle, but an American lion got back up on his feet and roared."

"Another cultist made an even deeper connection. 'He can stand defiant against an assassin one moment and call for national healing the next.'"

"In fact, he wasn't thinking about anybody else's safety," said Byrne. "He just popped up his head, waved his fist, and yelled 'fight.'"

He's Napoleon in a golf cart," said Jackson. "There's no doctor's report, and likely never will be, but I heard that the slug was only a wood splinter."

"The meeting was less a convention than a convocation."

"A MAGA congregation beatifying a gladiator who broke all Ten Commandments," said Byrne.

"Unfortunately, having performed his healing act in honeyed tones, he was stuck with the healing act."

"His theme of unity turned into a plea for his criminal convictions to be dropped."

"He actually said that the price of unity is to 'drop these witch hunts.'"

"He was a scofflaw trying to stay out of jail..."

"A self-styled Man on the Cross, tortured for our sins..."

"A Bible and Gold Sneaker salesman."

"Whose worshipers streamed out of the church carrying pre-printed MASS DEPORTATION NOW signs."

"Revenge and retribution are the Devil's catechism."

"It's an open secret. The Republican Party *is* the Donald."

Soon enough the audience was back to its comfort zone, booing and clapping as Trump criticized 'crazy Nancy Pelosi' and cheering as he rambled on about 'rapacious foreigners plundering our nation.'

"An omen of things to come might be that the Donald personally invited the chief of the Ultimate Fighting Championship to introduce him."

"Trump always treated politics as a blood sport."

"Once a bully boy, always a Devil."

"His VP pick looks as aimless as the guy at the bachelor party who doesn't know any of the groomsmen."

"Then came Hulk Hogan!"

"Sounding like a Disney version of a pro-wrestler giving a political speech."

"He riffed about 'real Americans' who'll be running wild the next four years—"

"—and 'gladiators' who'll lead them."

"Then in honour of the Donald's near-death experience, the Hulk ripped off his shirt, and flashed his bulbous biceps and a red Trump-Vance T-shirt. 'I know tough guys,' he said, 'and Donald Trump is the toughest of them all.'"

"Then he puffed his gorilla chest."

"The Donald blew him a kiss and pumped his fist."

"I got the impression," I said, "that every cultist believes that if Trump loses the next election it'll be because of fraud. 'Democrats want to cheat,' he said. 'They do it by opening the borders for aliens to vote.'"

"Republicans say they are building an army of poll watchers and observers to watch over the vote this year. They've also appointed a lawyer facing criminal charges in Arizona for her involvement in the fake electors scheme to head the party's litigation efforts," said Jackson.

"There are similar efforts to scrub the rolls in other

places, and voting rights groups have expressed concern sloppy practices could lead to eligible voters being removed."

"We need a nabob to call out the Donald's lies."

"Only a saint—and I didn't see any there—would draw attention to a devilish tongue."

"Amen to that," said Jackson.

"And amen to our discussion," I said.

"Dreamland beckons," said Jackson.

"An angel is calling?"

Back in my bed I brought up the news on my iPhone that the wannabe white-male assassin was in fact a twenty-year-old registered Republican. So maybe the shooting was just another cry for help from some badly adjusted youth who'd otherwise get the attention he craved by shooting up his teachers and schoolmates? So maybe it truly was a case of divine intervention? Maybe the gods were hoping to showcase the plight of the shooter and the scourge of guns in America. I turned off the bedside light and prayed for the sleep that knits up the raveled sleeve of care.

> *In my dream, a pistol-packing Reverend Billy Graham was preaching to a massive crowd. Behind him, his son Franklin, clad in shiny red tights, but otherwise naked save for a native American-Indian headdress, was performing in front of an altar, above which a Corpus Christi was spinning. Then Billy Graham pulled his sixgun from his halter and shot a golden bullet into Franklin's heart.*

A MAN OF TWO MINDS

First thing next morning, I checked the *New York Times* on my phone. Democrats were panicked and calling for Biden to quit the race. A leading Democratic strategist was publicly warning a 'landslide' if he didn't. Well, goodness. If a coup against Joe Biden succeeded, Republicans will be staking their future on a rapidly aging demagogue who was repudiated by voters only four years ago. I remembered the RNC cultists cheering, 'Joe Must Go! Joe Must Go! Joe Must Go!' Democrats might want to chant the very same message. Trump seemed to be anticipating that Democrats might do just that. Trump's entire campaign had been built around defeating 'Sleepy Joe'. He may soon have to pivot. But to whom? And against what? Be careful what you wish for. Trump may have had a brush with death, but he had not been reborn. He was just older and angrier, and more reliant on his odium of nickname hate and pitiless cunning.

After breakfast seemed as good a time as any to jot down my thoughts on JD Vance. I might even persuade a publisher to take it. He's what I managed to write...

JD VANCE PROFILE

Bio

James Donald Bowman—who changed his name to James David Vance in 2014—was born on August 2, 1984, in Middletown, Ohio. He is of Scots-Irish descent. His parents divorced when he was a toddler. Shortly afterward, Bowman was adopted by his mother's third husband, Bob Hamel, and had his name changed to James David Hamel. Vance's childhood was marked by poverty and abuse, and his mother struggled with drug addiction. Vance and his sister Lindsey were raised primarily by his maternal grandparents, whom they called "Mamaw and Papaw." His grandparents on both sides moved to Ohio from Kentucky's Appalachia.

After graduating high school he sought to put some structure in his life by joining the Marines. Upon release, with the support of the G.I. Bill, he attended Ohio State University and completed a bachelor's degree in political science and philosophy in 2019. Keenly attracted to politics, he served a stint working for Republican Senator John Cornyn. He then enlisted in the Marine Corps and served in Iraq, but became disillusioned with the political situation that fomented that war. That would seem to be the reason that, after returning to society, he created a non-profit 'to help disadvantaged children achieve their dreams.'

Key Influences

Sixteen years older than Vance, PayPal billionaire Peter Thiel was, and is, Vance's key mentor. They met at Yale when Thiel gave a speech that Vance says changed his life. Age-wise, Thiel fits that mold; more than a contemporary and less than a parent. Somewhere between a father surrogate and a Svengali.

In August 2019—four years after his wedding—lifelong evangelical JD Vance, was baptized into the Roman Catholic faith.

Vance credits his conversion to his exposure—via Thiel —to the writings of the French philosopher René Girard, whom Thiel studied under at Stanford University. Bear in mind that Girard is most famous for his theory of 'mimetic desire': that human beings imitate the desires of their peers, ultimately giving rise to rivalries and violent conflicts that are resolved by scapegoating a common enemy.

It seems no wonder that Vance zealously opposes abortion and believes a woman's place is in the home. And at every turn Vance's career has been funded by Thiel. Thiel actually introduced Vance to Trump. And, as you know, most recently Thiel marched Vance into Trump's presence, and urged him to make Vance his running mate.

Vance's other key influence seems to be his wife. She was born to immigrant Indian parents and was raised a Hindu. She studied law, had a stint with a law firm, then went on to clerk for none other than Supreme Court Chief Justice John Roberts and noted alcoholic Brett Kavanaugh. Vance married her in 2014 in Kentucky, in an interfaith marriage ceremony, which included a Christian Bible reading and a blessing by a Hindu pundit. She remains a practicing Hindu, and, some say, a Stepford wife.

Then in 2019, just four years after his wedding, Vance was baptized into the Catholicism of Thiel.

Attitude to Trump

In his former liberal incarnation Vance has said, 'I go back and forth between thinking Trump is a cynical asshole or that he's America's Hitler.' Indeed, he has also labeled Trump 'an idiot… cultural heroin… a noxious leader who is taking the white working class to a very dark place.'

But then, sighting greater opportunities within the Republican party, he became a Trumpster. So, noting that 'J.D. is kissing my ass,' Trump endorsed Vance in April 2022. In the Senate, he emerged standard-bearer of a movement of young conservatives waging culture wars. Vance has also said that if he had been in Mike Pence's shoes in 2021, he would not have certified the results of the 2020 election. He also called Trump's hush-money trial in New York a 'threat to American democracy.'

Conclusions

JD Vance is a classic overachiever, driven by the spurs of a rotten childhood and poverty. Given that at thirty years of age he changed his birth name from James Donald Bowen to James David Vance, he might also be a victim of the 'imposter syndrome.'

That said, his graduations from Ohio and Yale, and his significant writing talent, suggest a facile thinker who can hold several ideas at the same time.

The downside is that he customizes his opinions to advance his career. In fact, his overarching loyalty is to Svengalian Peter Thiel, whose key belief right now, as Thiel himself has expressed it, is that 'freedom is incompatible with democracy.' So, behind the façade, Vance is essentially a spineless sycophant of Trump. As a duo, Trump and Vance are essentially two peas in a pod. For sure, JD Vance is the man you bring in when you want to install a dictatorship.

I had hardly penned that piece when the curtain opened on a dramatically new political era...

PART TWO

REICHSTAG SCENT

Even on a good day Joe Biden looked feeble. Clearly, as Jackson noted, advancing age had unkindly restored his speech impediment. If you followed closely, what he had to say was wise. But the yesteryear ploys he'd learned to subdue his stutter merely made him sound even more confused, degrading his lines almost to pidgin English. And so he gave into reality. But who might replace him? Even among Democrats, Joe Biden's tawny female VP was not a unanimously popular choice. She also had a Jewish husband. But surely only a redneck would care about that? Kamala Harris was, of course, a dedicated, intelligent, overtly entertaining professional. Best of all, perhaps, she showcased the rapier debating skills that she had developed as a crown prosecutor. And, as luck would have it, she was also the anointed keeper of the one and only key to the Democratic campaign war chest. No argument there. In fact, a wave of elation flooded the republic. But how would Trump respond?

"One thing we can be sure of," said Byrne, "is that the Devil in Donald is spoiling for an uprising. He's all but said it over and over. In the minds of his cultists, the supposedly divine intervention to spare the life of Donald Trump, and his apparent acknowledgment of the Almighty—his Christ-like shedding of blood, his glorious fist waves and wild cries to fight—is all they need to justify anarchy. All it will take is another Reichstag fire."

"A Reichstag fire?" I said.

"Or something like it. The original 1933 Reichstag fire was an arson attack on the home of the German parliament in Berlin. Historians say it was a Nazi false flag operation. By the time police and firefighters arrived, the place was ablaze. The police searched inside the building and found and arrested

Marinus van der Lubbe, a Dutch Council Communist. Hitler blamed communist agitators for the blaze. Said they were plotting against the German government. Van der Lubbe and four communists got executed."

"So there really is no God?" said Jackson.

Byrne smiled. "Uunder a law introduced in 1998, Van der Lubbe was posthumously pardoned."

"Do you think Trump knew about the Reichstag?"

"They say kept a copy of *Mein Kampf* on his beside table."

"You mentioned a bouquet of justice," said Jackson. "Rumor has it that the Donald gives off an altogether unhappy aroma."

"Really?" said Byrne.

"Quoted people who'd whiffed it. Seems he's had it since the eighties, and might just be incontinent."

"Incontinent?" said Byrne.

"Seems someone from *The Apprentice* said so."

"Only behind his back." Jackson stifled a smile.

Byrne was riled. "There's no joking with the Devil. We need to see this as a signal." We all sighed. But the more I thought about it, the more I realized that Trump was not just mentally ill. "Yes, Byrne, you're right," I said. "Trump is what the *Diagnostic and Statistical Manual of Mental Disorders* calls a malignant narcissist."

"As a CEO he's on the ropes," said Jackson. "But I doubt he's ready to quit."

"He really is the Devil is what I say!"

So those were our final words. I put them out of mind. Or so I thought.

In my dream that night, I was trapped inside a set of revolving doors. I cried out for help, but no one could hear me. Then the floor beneath me opened, and I sank into a fiery tunnel.

STEEL MAGNOLIA

I met up with Byrne, Jackson, and Margot for an after-work drink at the front lounge and bar at Giorgio's on 21st Street.

"So, Kamala is surging in the polls," said Byrne, fondling his ginger ale.

Jackson took a sip from his Shiraz. "It's early days, but she's looking like a winner."

"And a leader, too?" I asked.

"Right now, she seems exactly the right person to trip the Donald. But if and when she wins, the power of the presidency will reveal her inner mettle."

"Do *you* think she has what it takes?" I said.

Jackson grinned. "As the Chinese proverb has it, 'to make prediction very difficult—especially regarding the future.'" He set his glass on the table. "So, in my humble opinion, past behavior is the key to a leader's future." He gathered himself. "Kamala Harris was born in Oakland, the progeny of a Jamaican father and an Indian mother, both immigrants. He became the first black scholar to be granted tenure at Stanford. The mother, a biologist and doctor, spent forty years researching cancer and ultimately changed the world." He showed a professional grin. "So Kamala had a lot to live up to."

"Trump says she's low-IQ—"

"—but hides his own transcripts," said Margot.

"Trump tries to pin that label on every opponent, especially smart women," I said.

Jackson continued. "In fact, Kamala graduated from Howard U, then UCLA Law. And then she became a prosecutor, District Attorney for San Francisco, Attorney General of California, a U.S. Senator—"

"—and capped it by running for President," said Byrne.

"You're saying she'll make a *great* president?" I asked. Jackson's inner leadership guru smiled again. "Her parents divorced when she was seven... So the greatest influence in her life became her dedicated, loving, high-achieving, single mother."

"So Kamala's a driven achiever, too?" said Margot.

"The big difference," said Jackson, "is that unlike her nurturing mother, Kamala chose to make her mark on violent criminals... so behind that laughing mask, she might just be an aggressive, steely, compulsive workaholic."

"That would explain the rumor that she's 'the boss from hell,'" said Byrne.

"Might not matter," said Jackson. "She'll be driven to make the world a fairer, better place—"

"—and she'll have formidable enemies scheming for her to fail," said Margot.

"So she might just be the Steel Magnolia America needs,"I said.

"I'm seeing a greater person than I ever dreamed she'd be,"said Byrne.

"Do you have a professional take on her running mate?"

"Give credit to Kamala for a savvy choice. My take is that she chose Tim Walz for three reasons. First, he very successfully branded the Donald as 'weird.'"

"That was a stroke of genius," said Byrne.

"The choice might have been unconscious, but it speaks to a deep understanding of the power of words."

"For sure it got under Trump's skin," said Margot.

"And, second, Walz shares Kamala's values. "He's an affable, empathetic leader who wants to pursue progressive policies that help the lives of everyday Americans." Jackson took another sip from his Shiraz, then set the glass back on the table. "And, third, Walz has a great heart. Soldiers, students, and athletes all look up to him. He's a small-town guy, who did a series of odd jobs after high school, from building grain silos to processing mortgage loans. He enlisted in the Army National Guard at age seventeen and served for twenty-four years."

"Vance accused him of 'stolen valor,'said Byrne.

"The trick for Vance is to poke holes in the perception that Walz's military service signals masculinity," said Jackson.

"That it confers street cred on men who wear the uniform," I said.

"Vance's saying that if Walz can't fight for himself, he can't fight for us, either?" said Margot.

Jackson grinned. "As the running mate of Captain Bone Spurs, Vance is a dedicated hypocrite." He drew a breath. "Walz's career speaks to his authenticity and empathy. He taught on a native Indian reservation, enrolled at a State college, taught English in China, then landed a job as a small-town high school social studies teacher.

"He's a gun owner," said Byrne.

"And a great marksman, too," I said. "He used to have an A- rating from the NRA. But after mass shootings in Las Vegas and at the Parkland high school, he saw the light, sent back the NRA campaign contributions, and now they've given him an F-rating."

"He's had a great political career, in both Congress and as state governor," said Jackson. "In both life and politics he's showing himself to be a leader who truly does know how to recruit and coach a winning team."

"The good news is the passionate crowds that are coming to hear Kamala and Tim," said Byrne.

"They're driving the Orange Guy crazy," said Margot.

"No kidding," said Jackson.

"We could usefully talk a whole lot more about that

fellow's mental condition—"

"—and what to do about it," said Byrne.

Jackson glanced to his watch, and then to Margot. "But time has flown."

"As it always does when you're having fun," said Margot.

And so our meeting ended. Happily, the Democratic National Convention and the Hush Money sentencing were coming up fast. Trump's reptilian cunning was also racing.

DNC HIGH

So we—Jackson and Margot and Byrne and I—agreed to watch the Democratic National Convention separately, then meet to talk about it at Giorgio's. Here's how our conversation went...

Margot jumped right in:"This is not a normal election."

"If it was in a courtroom it would be," said Jackson.

"It's the only time in American history that a crown prosecutor and a convicted felon have appeared on the same ballot," said Byrne.

"That felon is also a serial sexual abuser," said Margot.

"And a pathological liar," I said. "He even claimed that nobody showed up at a live-streamed, ten-thousand person Harris-Walz rally in Michigan, that it was all AI."

"He's laying the ground for rejecting the results when he loses," said Jackson.

"Given everyone's sky-high hopes, I worried that Kamala might not live up to the hype," said Margot.

"But she delivered a coupe de grace," I said. "The final session was like a nervous laugh after outfoxing an angry bandit."

"Anyone worried about her campaign can relax," said Margot.

"But glee is premature," said Jackson. "And the polls might prove more stubborn than we might think."

"The plan," said Byrne, "is to garner the votes of young people and minorities who were apathetic about Biden."

"And every pro-choice woman," said Margot.

"Kamala has inspired voters and campaigned in the shortest imaginable time," said Jackson.

"And in unprecedented situations," said Byrne.

"She has to be more than a younger Joe," said Margot.

"She's still not laid out much of an immigration plan," said Jackson.

"Not so," said Margot. "In fact she said Trump tanked the bipartisan immigration bill."

"All well and good," I said. "But what's her vision for *legal* immigrants?"

"Like her parents," said Jackson. "And what about mass deportations? Will she simply go with whatever polls best?"

"Right now Trump seems like a punch drunk boxer who wants to get out of the ring," I said.

"His sidekick isn't helping either," said Jackson. "The Donald is a one-trick pony. He'll just ratchet up his racist rhetoric."

"And misogynistic machinations," said Margot.

"Kamala seems wise to the idea that pointing to glass ceilings is a needless distraction," said Jackson.

"She rarely says she'd be our first female president," said Byrne.

"Unlike Hillary's 'I'm with Her' campaign," I said.

"I worry about what might still happen before the election," said Margot.

"A stock-market crash, a Middle East war, a Putin victory in Ukraine—"said Jackson.

"—or a nasty happening right here," I said.

"The lack of an Israel–Hamas cease-fire is also an open sore."

"She's onto it," said Margot. "'Now's the time to get a hostage deal *and* a ceasefire deal done' is what she said."

"She took just one step to the left of Biden," said Jackson. "And that might not quell the street protests.

"Fanaticism and myopia are two sides of the same coin," I said.

"The convention was always inspiring," said Margot.

"But it's only the end of an opening act," said Jackson. "Republican voters are more stubborn than anyone who attends a banquet for the Democratic faithful."

"Trump's looking weaker by the day," I said.

"I'm not sure 'the other guy is worse' is a great argument for swing voters," said Jackson.

"Kamala absorbed the great vibes and then created glittering jewels for Democrats to gaze on," said Byrne.

"The higher you rise the harder you fall," I said.

"As Biden learned mere weeks ago," said Jackson.

Margot had the last word. "What I say is, the higher you rise the harder you hit 'em."

GALA AWARDS

Byrne was on the phone and breathing hard. "Such terrible things are happening that I don't know which to share first. But I'll try." He paused. "First, I guess you heard about the J6 Awards Gala at Trump's Bedminster golf club?"

"I think it's a fundraiser?"

"Right! Fifty thousand dollars per table for legal fees for J6 defendants. But they're framing it as—let me read it for you—'a tribute to all J6 defendants who have shown incredible courage and sacrifice.'"

"Trump promised to pardon convicted J-Sixers, including those who assaulted officers, so that's no surprise."

"He calls them 'hostages' actually." Byrne sighed. "It's being set up by the wife of a Tennessee deputy sheriff serving five years in prison for attacking Capitol police. Trump is an invited speaker and Giuliani is confirmed. Trump has already appeared with some of the defendants at private events at his properties." He drew a deep breath. "He's even opened campaign events with a recording of defendants singing the national anthem from their jail cells."

"A choir of jailbirds?"

"One of the organizers is serving seven years for breaking a window at the capital with a tomahawk, then pelting officers with a wooden desk drawer, a flagpole, a metal walking stick, and a broken wooden pole. And..." Byrne took a long pause, "he messaged a friend and actually said, Susan 'I'm not over this election, and I have murder in my heart and head.'"

"Not a happy camper."

"That's not the worst of it. On the same day as the fund-raiser, a Washington Federal District Court hearing will determine how the SCOTUS presidential immunity ruling applies to our newfound King."

"That could turn out to be a real problem."

"Trump also shared a social media post implying that Kamala owed her political rise to sexual favours."

"Par for the course with him."

"What I'm most perturbed about, however, is that Trump is inviting QAnon cultists into the battle. He reposted: 'WWG1WGA! RETRUTH IF YOU AGREE.'"

"Huh?"

"It's a QAnon acronym; 'where we go one, we go all.' He also reposted 'NCSWIC'—Nothing Can Stop What Is Coming."

"Look on the bright side," I said. "The latest Reuters poll has Harris with a four-point lead."

Byrne paused for so long that I thought the call might have dropped. But no, he came back, this time calmly. "Ah, Paul, these rotten things—the J6 Gala awards, the SCOTUS ruling that Trump's a King, the QAnon reposts—they truly are the work of the Devil." I know you don't believe in Satan, but these things are *evil*... and we absolutely must judge a tree by the fruit that it bears." He paused. "I have to go now, but do me a favor, at least think about it."

And so I did. Despite, or maybe because of, Byrne's predilection to see a devil behind every tree, I concluded that the bottom was dropping out of Trump's campaign, and his 'Awards Gala' would surely fail. The vaunted defendants and 'hostages' would surely shrink from being filmed, yet again, by the media, or from being charged again by the Justice Department. But Trump could also surely see the writing on the wall. If so, he knew that to escape a prison sentence, he absolutely must win back the Presidency. And to achieve that, he'd need to out-debate Kamala. Failing that he'd have to foment another civil uprising. But which would come first?

FIGHT OR FLIGHT?

It was getting closer. I fell to obsessing over the decisions that Judge Juan Merchan was facing for Trump's September 18th sentencing. Disguising my anxiety, I grabbed my iPhone and called Jackson. "I'm just wondering," I said, "what your take might be on the outcome of the New York Hush Money hearing?"

"I'm flattered you'd ask." He paused. "Well, if the Donald was in the dock and I were the judge I'd say, 'you've been found guilty by a jury of your peers of thirty-four felonies. You've also been fined time and again for breaching the terms of your gag order. And from the beginning of this trial right up until this moment, you've shown absolutely no remorse... Any other such convicted criminal would be sentenced to jail time. And no-one is above the law. So the ruling of this court is that you be sentenced to serve three months on Rikers Island jail.'" Jackson paused. "The question in this moment for the judge is whether to lock the Donald up immediately, or let him continue his election campaign by suspending the sentence until after the November election."

I thought about that for a moment. "I'm sure it's wise to assume that Trump is aware of both scenarios. He also knows that the latest polls are forecasting him to lose. My head also tells me that he's so desperate to avoid serving prison time—or wind up looking like a 'loser'—that he'll find a way to skip the Hush Money sentencing."

Jackson thought for a few seconds. "You read the piece I sent you on Gonnabee CEOs, right?"

"Indeed."

"So, when, like Icarus, they rise above their talents, what mostly happens is that Gonnabees suffer what seems to be a serious illness that immediately entitles them to head for a hospital bed." He paused. "The problem, they say, is that they were working too hard to ensure the welfare of the so-called team." He sighed. "They may express remorse for this so-called failing, but they never feel even an ounce of shame."

"No remorse?"

"I guess, as a prison reformer, you have a professional interest in that kind of thing? I'll rummage through my files and email you something you might find helpful."

So that was the Leadership Guru's opinion. I mulled it carefully. But what if Trump was just another corporate CEO? His was a family business, right? He'd skipped the journey from the mailroom to the boardroom, and was arbitrarily appointed by Chief of the Kingdom by his father. So what might Donald do to dodge the pain of seeming to be, in the pact he struck with his old man, not ever to be judged for what he surely was, an outright loser? Might he not, as psychotics do, just disappear into his head? Or, might he find a way to create a distraction. He's a pitiless bully, remember, so that would mean, as we'll soon see, a *nasty* distraction.

THE LONG VIEW

Jackson was on the phone. "You heard the news right? Judge Merchan has pushed the hush-money sentencing from September twenty all the way to November twenty-sixth."

"Just two days before Thanksgiving?!"

"He's taken a longer view than anyone quite realizes."

"Did he give a reason?"

"Kind of. He said that given that the election was imminent, and given the Supreme Court decision that the Donald is now akin to an emperor, the issues were complex."

"So, one way or another the SCOTUS gave Trump yet another get-out-of-jail-free card."

"Not quite. That card is only valid until November twenty-six."

"Time enough to cause some mischief."

"Maybe not."

"Really?"

"The judge has delivered the Donald a double whammy."

"How so?"

"He's *also* delayed his judgment on whether the SCOTUS immunity ruling applies to the New York hush-money trial. He'll rule on that a couple of days prior to November 26.

"Huh?"

"What that means is that the Donald won't have any time to get SCOTUS to help him out. He's fresh out of legal appeals until after the election."

"So he'll have no reason to play *any* kind of victim—"

"—and absolutely no excuse if he loses the election."

"I'm sure he'll find one!"

"In the increasingly unlikely event that the Donald wins the election, on the facts of the case the Judge will still have to sentence him to prison time."

"He'll find a way to get out that!"

"And never forget, this is *not* a federal case, so even if the Donald becomes our forty-seventh president he won't be able to pardon himself."

"'From your lips to God's ears,' as Byrne might say."

Speaking of the Devil, immediately after ending the conversation, I called Byrne to share the news and get his take. He was, as usual, forthright, "Ah, Paul. How many times do you have to see it? Trump's inner Devil is the one who has taken the long view. Yet again, for all the world to see, the Devil has found a way to spare Donald from the ignominy of a stint inside a prison on this planet. And, mark my words, his inner Devil will find a way do it again."

A SMACK IN THE MOUTH

For the debate between Kamala and Donald, I met with Byrne and Hassan at Jackson and Margot's loft. I caught a sweet scent from the vase of red and yellow tulips on the coffee table. We gathered, as before, around that console laden with a bottle of Pellegrino, a ginger ale, an uncorked crimson Primitivo, a Pouilly-Fuissé, and a bowl of seasoned, potato chips. The television was on but the volume was off.

"So how do we think this'll go?" said Jackson.

"It'll be a win for Kamala," said Margot.

"You're sure?" I said.

"Trump posted this quote from an admirer," said Byrne, reading from his iPad. "'Donald Trump is the greatest political debater in American History.'"

"We shall soon enough see," said Margot.

Jackson held up the red and white wines. "Does anybody want to help us sip these lovely drops?"

"Pellegrino for me," said Hassan.

"And since it matches the color of my hair, I'll imbibe the ginger ale," said Byrne.

I joined Jackson with the crimson Primitivo. Margot opted for the Pouilly-Fuissé.

We raised our glasses in a toast.

"To democracy," said Jackson.

"Long may it reign," I said.

"To absent friends," whispered Hassan.

"To a happy outcome," said Byrne.

"May the best woman win," said Margot.

We clinked and sipped.

Byrne looked to Jackson. "Margot said you used to be a champion debater, so do you have any clues?"

Hassan nodded. "Trump outfoxed Hillary and Biden—"

"—and every GOP contender," I said.

Jackson was momentarily lost in thought. "Television audiences don't remember much. They judge by looks, not content, delivery not logic. Winners are adept at making one key idea stick in the mind of the audience."

"Creating memes?" said Byrne

"Yes—and memes don't need to be rational," said Jackson.

"Trump is already undercutting the election results," said Byrne. "Over the weekend, he threatened to lock up the so-called cheats who he still insists stole his forty-sixth Presidency. And just this afternoon he insisted that congressional Republicans vote down a pending measure to keep the federal government open, weirdly claiming that Democrats were using the resolution to secretly enable illegal aliens to vote."

"The Donald is a master of promoting fallacies," said Jackson.

"Like his lie that pro-choice advocates are executing live babies," said Margot.

"Or that an invasion of aliens is poisoning our blood," I said. "He called them thugs and vermin and promised he'd root them out."

"They're Adolf Hitler quotes," said Byrne. "Trump's speechwriter seems all-too well versed in Third Reich doctrines."

"Never forget the power of an apparently spontaneous zinger," I said. "All anyone remembers of his debate with Jimmy Carter was Ronald Reagan's one-liner, 'there you go again.'"

"Called Jimmy a liar right to his face," said Hassan.

"And the audience loved it," said Margot.

"So watch the opening very closely. Right from the get-go the Donald's tactic is a blend of sucker-punch and insult. I don't know which he'll conjure, and, until he steps onto the platform, I don't think he does either."

"I'm sure Kamala has a plan," said Margot.

"Right!" said Hassan. "But as Mike Tyson says, 'every fighter has a plan until somebody smacks him in the mouth.'"

"So, dodge the opening sucker punch. And, since Hassan mentioned Mike Tyson, I'd share the advice that coach Angelo Dundee shared with every boxer at the opening bell of a championship bout, 'It's just hard sparring, and you're in charge.'"

Margot topped our glasses as Jackson stepped forward and turned the volume up.

"And here's that opening bell right now," said Hassan.

"Wow!" said Margot, as Kamala entered stage left, strolled across the platform with her hand outstretched.

"She's commanding the Donald to shake her hand," said Jackson.

"She just delivered the sucker punch," said Hassan.

We watched the rest of the debate in mostly stunned but elated silence.

When it was over, Jackson and Margot refilled our glasses, but this time Hassan opted for the Primitivo.

Jackson silenced TV volume, and we relaxed.

"Who says a elfin woman can't outfox an obese ogre?" said Margot.

"She was Davida and he was Goliath," said Byrne.

"She smacked Bully Boy in the mouth," said Hassan

Byrne pointed to his iPad. "Historian Michael Beschloss just said Kamala delivered one of the most successful ever Presidential debate performances."

"Age got the better of Biden," said Jackson. "But this time, the lost old man on the stage was the Donald."

Margot pretended to hide a smile. "She unwrapped the

long red tie from his groin and exposed his tiny crazy uncle," she said.

We mostly failed to stifle our laughter.

"He called her a "Marxist and said she's worst Vice-President in American history," said Byrne.

"And that's exactly how he fell into every trap that Kamala laid," I said. "He ranted about his court cases, doubled down on his election denialism, insulted both Kamala and Biden, and bragged about how he's friends with Putin."

"Which is why he refused to answer whether it was in America's interests for Ukraine to win the war with Russia," said Jackson.

"Putin's got something over him," said Hassan.

"Or maybe Trump has unresolved father issues," I said.

"Whatever," said Margot. "But what could be crazier than ranting about Haitian refugees supposedly gobbling down taxpayer pets?"

Hassan raised his hand. "Maybe his line about Kamala arranging transgender operations on jailed aliens."

"What in heaven's name was he talking about?" said Byrne.

"No one knows, not even him," said Margot.

"Which was precisely Kamala's point," I said.

"He's a master of nonsensical distraction," said Jackson. "His response to overturning Roe v. Wade became a screed about Kamala executing babies."

"And insisting every American wanted to overturn Roe v. Wade," said Byrne.

"Kamala pounced on that," said Margot. "Called it insulting, and said she'd do everything in her power to stop what she cleverly called 'Trump abortion bans.'"

"Her passion was authentic and memorable."

"Her *most* memorable line was 'It's important to remind the former president that you're not running against Joe Biden, you're running against me.'"

"She floored him with that punch," said Hassan.

"Beat him at his own game," said Margot.

"The Donald created himself in a reality television show," said Jackson. "As mentioned, he knows how to keep the red light on the top of the video camera gleaming. He can put on an act for local yokels. But he's a performer not a serious actor. He let it all hang out and Kamala presented him the rope he needed to lynch himself."

"If we judge the debate by looks and delivery, she delivered in cool and cogent prosecutor mode, and when listening to his playbook she seemed ironically bemused by his antics," said Jackson. "Whereas the Donald played his 'A-game' playbook of lies, insults, distractions and denials. When she was talking he kept his lip zipped, but looked sullen and angry and petulant. Even when he managed a smile,all it came off looking like a tight-lipped, toothless smirk." He drew a deep sigh. "Maybe none of it will matter," he said. "The polls are saying that Kamala's honeymoon might be ending. And that in most battleground states the race is a dead heat."

"Maybe Trump's crazy uncle act is baked into the polls and every voter has a made-up mind," said Margot.

"She knocked him out of the ring," said Hassan. "Hey, look," he pointed to the screen. "Trump's gone to the spin room and he's working the refs."

Jackson stepped forward, turned up the volume, and absorbed the scene. "He's saying the polls are in and everyone's saying he won."

"He *says he* cleaned *her* clock!" said Hassan.

"And that it was his greatest debate ever," said Margot.

I shared a look with Byrne. "Can you believe it?" I said. He shook his head, shrugged, and said nothing.

Byrne and I headed out into the comforting autumn night and strolled up Broadway to the 23rd Street subway station.

"Another great night," I said.

He stopped stock still and held my gaze. "I'm not sure that you guys saw what I saw," he said."

"What I saw in full color on that screen," I said, "was an unprepared felon face off against a professional prosecutor whose every word and glance and smile and gesture destined his demise." Byrne touched a hand to his brow as I pressed on. "And in the spin room I couldn't quite decide whether that orange felon was working the referees or actually believed his own lies, in which case he might be going crazy."

"That's not what I saw," said Byrne. We shared a glance to the lights within the iconic, ever-memorable Flatiron building. "What I saw," he said, "was a devil engaged in a battle with an angel of light." He sighed. "Oh Paul, I know you still don't believe me. But think back." He drew a breath and raised his palms. "As Kamala gracefully ascended, Trump's skin became a stickier, bubblier shade of red-hot coals and ultimately burst into the hate-filled proclamation that Haitians devour our lovable pets." He glanced away then back. "As you've heard me say so many times before, the devil looks after his own. So, Trump's spin-room strongman spun a litany of lies for the benefit of the cultists that his inner Devil is intending to enlist to upend the election before it ever begins."

Back in my studio bed, I reran Byrne's words. So I saw an angry man and he saw a scheming Satan? Maybe there are more things twixt heaven and earth than philosophy or science can explain. The universal, undying appeal of *The Twilight Zone* TV series might support the human inclination to believe in the supernatural. But, alas, the safe bet is that we are alone in this cosmos and governed by random events—and that the meaning of life is that it ends. So make the most of what we may spend before we too into the dust descend?

> *I dreamed of a boxing ring and a sparring bout between the Prince of Darkness and Zophiel the Angel of God's Knowledge, both of whom were wearing headgear so puffy that they were effectively blind. As they flailed away at each other, the gloves of the Angel bloodied the face of the Devil. Then the bell sounded and the referee grabbed and held up Lucifer's claw and proclaimed him the winner. Then a naked lady-of-the-night appeared and paraded a sign that read The End Is Nigh.*

BITTER PILL

Byrne was on the phone again. "Trump blamed Joe and Kamala for the assassination attempt. He said Kamala's rhetoric inspired the shooter."

"In fact she condemned it."

"So did Biden."

"Trump told Doctor Phil they weaponized the FBI."

"*Doctor Phil?* I'm pretty sure he's a Trumpster."

"And now Trump has tweeted that they forced him to take a bullet for democracy."

"So what else is new? Back in the day, when the FBI went into Mar-a-Lago to retrieve the classified documents he stole, Trump accused them of being locked and loaded and ready to kill him."

"I remember. Trump was out of town, and, for their own safety, standard procedure required them to be armed."

"It's all part of Trump's playbook. He's talking to his base. He wants to put them in a fighting mood. He wants them to do his fighting for him."

"You might be right," said Byrne. "His Inner Devil wants them to fight for a hellish victory."

REMORSE

I don't believe that some imaginary graybeard in the sky answers our prayers. But I do believe in the Jungian concept of *synchronicity*, which I think boils down to the idea that when one door closes another one opens. Anyway, I was absentmindedly pondering whether Trump ever felt remorse for anything he did or said, when an email addressed to Byrne and me came in from Jackson.

> Hi there, Paul:
>
> As a prison teacher, I always found remorse a subject of special interest. I include a session on it in my Eagles program. Just to be clear, I have always shied from telling anyone that the road to salvation runs through the town of Remorse. I think some people feel it and some people don't. Anyway, for what it might be worth, here's the PDF I promised...

I often use this quote from Eugene O'Neill's play, *Long Day's Journey Into Night*: "*None of us can help the things life has done to us. They're done before you realize it, and once they're done they come between you and what you like to be, and you have lost your true self forever.*" So here's an apposite poem by a twenty-five year-old who still had 15 years of his sentence to serve...

> *Who am I?*
> *What have I done?*
> *I can't believe I did that.*
> *What have I become?*
> *Why are those guys oozing red?*
> *That one looks just like he's dead.*
> *They're staring at me, everyone.*
> *Wherever did I get this gun?*

So, here was a young man waking from a dream and stepping into a nightmare situation. Yes indeed, 15 years still to serve...

A lengthy incarceration is a subtle and relentless form of early death. A short stint in jail can be a learning experience. Indeed, I often commend it to my friends. To serve serious time without the nourishment of hope and change, however, is only to be wished upon enemies. Isolation from loved ones then becomes akin to water torture. One may stoically deny the inner pain, but the unrelenting dripping away of the days and nights atrophies both mind and heart. Most long servers are aware of the syndrome and make serious attempts to thwart it. "Do the time," they say, "don't let the time do you." But Father Time has never so far been arrested. Hence Dr. Seuss's question: "How did it get so late so soon? It's night before it's afternoon. December is here before it's June. My goodness how the time has flown. How did it get so late so soon?" Happily, with the passage of time, brave long servers discover hidden treasures of the soul. Hence this contribution by my friend, Richard…

> So, what is remorse? It's a stepping-stone to growth—real growth, honest to goodness, once and forever change. I came to realize that I'd been blind to all the harm I'd caused. I've seen with open eyes that truly remorseful ex-offenders like me *show* our remorse. Real remorse is more than a feeling. Saying "I'm sorry"is a good start but not enough. If we're truly remorseful we *act*. I don't mean just looking backwards and shaking our heads in wonderment that we were the benumbed zombie who did those terrible things. Yes, we *will* look back and shake our heads. But when a remorseful person *acts*, he makes good and by giving back. We set about renewing our communities. We become productive, law-abiding citizens. We *show* our children *right doings*. We make sure they get a decent education. We set them onto right roads. If you talk but don't act, remorse is just a word.

I'm sure you liked that piece. So here's another, this time from a lifer, and rather more complex…

It was late at night in Central Park. He was lying there, close

to the wall of the park, and under a streetlight. I stepped
up and took a close look. He was old, ragged and dirty,
and snoring with his mouth open. I had no reason to do
it, but I did. I strangled him until he stopped breathing.
And I wandered back home. I woke up early next morning
and he was on my mind. So I returned to the scene of the
crime. Yes, he was still lying there. But this time he seemed
to be staring at me. I stepped forward, closed his eyelids,
and turned to head back home. In that moment I glanced
backwards and took a last look. His left eyelid had opened
again. I reached into my pocket, found a quarter and gently
laid it over his left eye, and turned again to head back home.
Again I glanced back. His right eye seemed to be staring at
me. I grabbed another quarter from my pocket and flicked
it toward that eye. To my surprise, it landed perfectly. So
I headed home. I felt no remorse for that crime. But here
today I look back in amazement. Did I commit that heinous
crime? No! Surely not. It must have been the callous act of a
stranger I never met. But No, yet again. That stranger truly
was me. It happened thirty years ago but I'm not asking
for sympathy. I'll just say it again, and you may or may not
believe me. These days, this just seems to be the heartless act
of a stranger I have never met.

If the universe dispenses justice, the Donald will serves a
stint in prison. And, if synchronicity is real, then perhaps
looking for some escapist reading, he'll wind up in the the
prison library, and grab a copy of Raymond Chandler's
novel *The Long Goodbye* and read these lines…

In jail a man has no personality. He is a minor disposal
problem and a few entries on reports. Nobody cares who
loves or hates him, what he looks like, what he did with
his life. Nobody reacts to him unless he gives trouble. All
that is asked of him is that he go quietly to the right cell
and remain quiet when he gets there. There is nothing to
fight against, nothing to be mad at. A good jail is one of the
quietest places in the world. Life in jail is in suspension.

Just saying…

BLAZING PAN

I looked up. "JD spoke the quiet part out loud—" I said.

"—that the Donald is the second coming of Adolf Hitler?"

"Vance is an albatross around Trump's neck," said Byrne.

"He's also broken the first rule of power, 'Never Outshine the Master.' The Donald doesn't care whether he's a heel or a hero; he just wants to keep all eyes on himself."

"So he'll find a way to cut the albatross free."

"Unless you have a suggestion, right now Vance's VP status is locked in," said Jackson.

"I'll say it again; the *Diagnostic and Statistical Manual of Mental Disorders* defines Trump as a malignant narcissist. As such, no psychotherapist can change him."

"He's a pitiless bully for whom there is no cure,"echoed Jackson. "That's why, when he was just thirteen years old, his own father sent him off to board at a hellish military academy," said Jackson. "Made him take a trip on a grimy public train to get there, too."

"Out of the frying pan into the fire. The errant son just learned to be a better bully." I said. "So the Donald only has two options. He can either pay Vance off, or..."

"Or?" said Byrne.

"Do something nasty."

"Like?"

"A distraction so nasty it'll create a civil uprising."

"How might he set that up?" said Byrne.

I only needed to think for a moment. "He could maybe start," I said, "by hiring a mentally disturbed guy with a gun to shoot his failing running mate."

"You have quite an imagination," said Jackson.

"Desperate people do desperate things."

Byrne jumped in. "Wait a minute you guys," he said, "I might have something." He foraged through his satchel and came up with a piece of paper. "So let me just preface what I'm about to say with some lines from Don Miguel Ruiz—who you might remember was a surgeon before becoming a writer." He delivered the lines calmly ...

> People like to say that the conflict is between good and evil. The real conflict is between truth and lies. And there are forces that promote evil. We must oppose their distorted values by promoting human understanding and compassion. Otherwise, we join ranks with the brute beast and get in line as passive witnesses to the next generation of dictators and perpetrators of evil and lies.

Byrne folded the quote and set it back into his pocket. Then he shared a serious look, first with Jackson, then with me. "So let me share *my* truth." He squeezed his palms together. "You may scoff, but on the basis of my research, I have to conclude that Trump is possessed by the Devil. Yes, you can chaff, but I truly believe, deep in my soul, that nothing short of an exorcism will drive Lucifer to leave. And so, for heaven's sake, we must act."

I raised an eyebrow.

We shall see...

HITLER'S DOG

As you might expect, our conversation re devilish behavior sparked Byrne to do more research and send me this intriguing email next morning.

> My take on Trump's double down on his lie that Haitian immigrants in Springfield are eating pets is that someone on Trump's staff has been reading up on the rise of Germany's Third Reich.
>
> In his 1925 book Mein Kampf Hitler was blatant about his plan to foment anti-semitism to become an exalted German Fuhrer. *People could be induced to believe colossal lies, he said, because they couldn't believe that any leader 'could have the impudence to distort the truth so infamously.'*
>
> It's all straight out of Trump's Inner Devil's playbook. Read the attached Mein Kampf excerpt and you know what I mean...

But it remained for the Jews, with their unqualified capacity for falsehood, and their fighting comrades, the Marxists, to impute responsibility for the downfall precisely to the man who alone had shown a superhuman will and energy in his effort to prevent the catastrophe which he had foreseen and to save the nation from that hour of complete overthrow and shame.

By placing responsibility for the loss of the world war on the shoulders of Ludendorff they took away the weapon of moral right from the only adversary dangerous enough to be likely to succeed in bringing the betrayers of the Fatherland to Justice.

All this was inspired by the principle – which is quite true within itself – that in the big lie there is always a certain force of credibility; because the broad masses of a nation are always more easily corrupted in the deeper strata of their emotional nature than consciously or voluntarily;

and thus in the primitive simplicity of their minds they more readily fall victims to the big lie than thc small lie, since they themselves often tell small lies in little matters but would be ashamed to resort to large-scale falsehoods.

It would never come into their heads to fabricate colossal untruths, and they would not believe others could have the impudence to distort the truth so infamously. Even though the facts which prove this to be so may be brought clearly to their minds, they will still doubt and waver and will continue to think there may be some other explanation. For the grossly impudent lie always leaves traces behind it, even after it has been nailed down, a fact which is known to all expert liars in this world and to all who conspire together in the art of lying.

—Adolf Hitler, Mein Kampf, vol. I, ch. X

So, yes, Kamala and most everybody else laughed when Trump said it, but it wasn't by accident that Trump blurted out his lie about Haitians eating Ohio pets. Trump was and is committed to using that big lie in an underlying appeal to racists of all stripes. When he refers to immigrants stealing black jobs he's a Caucasian Fuhrer reminding his economically left-behind, pink brothers of how tawny refugees are worsening their own job losses to people of the 'wrong' ethnicity. To be fair, George H.W. Bush won his 1988 by showcasing the probation of African-American Willie Horton. And senate leader Mitch McConnell ran flagrantly racist campaigns that blended Obama's darkened image with hordes of black invaders bursting through our borders. Every streetwise politician knows that racism has a broad appeal—especially to those who seem to shun it. Misogyny too, of course.

BLAME GAME

All the while I was reading the *Guardian* piece on the second Trump assassination attempt I was expecting Byrne to call. And he did. "What you make of this latest shooting by Ryan Routh?" he asked.

"I'm thinking," I said, "that he's a fifty-eight-year-old politically fickle white guy with a borderline personality disorder and a craving for attention and fame."

"Not unlike Donald Trump?"

"That may be the attraction."

"Huh?"

"It might just be a case of unconscious projection. I'm thinking he apprehended his own faults in his former hero—he voted for Trump in 2016—then hated what he saw, and succumbed to an unconscious compulsion to kill him, thereby also garnering the fame he craved."

"Not unlike Judas betraying Christ for thirty pieces of silver?"

"Exactly. But this should've grown out of his immature compulsions thirty years ago. I'm also struck that he endorsed the presidential bid of someone reputed to be Putin's Manchurian candidate."

"Tulsi Gabbard? I remember Hillary Clinton saying something to that effect."

"Freudians might say that Ryan Routh was attempting to become his own man by killing his father and hoping for his mother to shower him with love and sexual favors."

Byrne sounded wary. "I'm not sure you'd like to be quoted saying that."

Ah, Byrne. Historians rummage for the truth but all too often overlook it "That nugget got Sigmund Freud into trouble, too." A thought came to me. "So perhaps it's as true as that 'love that dare not speak its name' line that Oscar Wilde cited in his first trial."

"Oscar was witty, but not always truthful."

"Do you have something like a truth of your own?"

"I'm not sure you'll like my point of view. But I'll share it anyway." His words were calm and rational, not at all the tone one might expect from a conservative cleric. "Ryan Routh might seem a rebel without a cause, but so does JD Vance. The difference is that Vance has chosen the side of evil, and Routh is mostly a good man spiritually, but ill-fated." He drew a deep breath. "So, yet again, the Devil himself has intervened and spared Donald Trump from an assassination attempt." I sensed the message that was coming. "The Devil also loaded Trump's brain and mouth with the thoughts and words with which to inspire his cultists to descend into the streets and foment another insurrection."

I doubted the wisdom of challenging that perception .

After we ended the call I phoned Jackson and shared my take on Routh and wondered whether he saw things differently.

"Right now I'm not sure of anything," he said. "Yes, Routh seems a mentally unstable character whose erratic political views and private life suggest a troubled upbringing. So that *might* all we need to know."

"But?"

"Call me crazy, but my other hunch is that this misguided fellow might just be one of Putin's useful idiots."

"But he's a Ukraine supporter."

"It seems that way. But he's unreliable, to say the least. Anyway, if you were Putin and were in mind of finding someone to create the kind of distraction that removed Trump's rotten debate performance from the public mind, and which might ultimately help Trump to get his gun-nut cultists to create a civil uprising, then Ryan Routh might be just the man you'd choose.

"But would this fame seeker risk his life just to create a distraction?"

"If you were Putin, you'd say the whole thing was only rigged to get attention, that there'd be no actual assassination, and that he'd have a safe getaway, and you would promise to pay more than enough to pay off his debts and live the life of Riley."

"That is definitely *not* the way it all turned out."

"Putin wouldn't care. He's a cold-blooded killer. So long as the Donald goes on creating more American chaos, sacrificing one more useful idiot wouldn't matter to him.

After we ended the call. I checked the news. Wow! Trump was ratcheting up the blame game. Both assassination attempts were caused by the "Communist Left Rhetoric" coming from Biden and Harris, "the enemy within...who'll do whatever it takes to stop us... bullets are flying and it will only get worse!"

SAFE BET

I met with Jackson, Margot, and Byrne for a coffee at Giorgio's. "I'm hearing from a well-placed fellow at Fox," said Jackson, "that a meeting of evangelical leaders has been urgently scheduled at Mar-a-Lago to pray for heavenly forces to help the Donald win the election."

Byrne jumped right in. "So let's find a way to get into that meeting with someone graced with the special powers to drive out the Trump's nesting Devil with historically proven prayers, gestures, symbols, sacred images, and sacramentals."

I stepped into the silence. "I figure that Trump already knows that even if he loses the election, Judge Merchan will sentence him to serious prison time. So how might the devil save him?"

"Satan always finds a way," said Byrne.

"It's a safe bet that the Donald knows Judge Merchan will jail him," said Jackson. "So he'll likely create some kind of civil uprising, either before the election or before he has to front up in court."

"He's already prepared the ground to do just that," I said. "When he loses the election—or maybe even before that happens—he'll say that everything was rigged."

"His hard-core cultists will agree on that."

"And a bunch of them are gun-toters spoiling for a fight," said Jackson.

"He'll pump his fist and order them order them to fight, fight, fight," said Byrne.

"He might well get another insurrection going," said Margot.

"And if and when they make him Fuhrer he'll give them government jobs," said Jackson.

"But meantime he'll feed them lies and MAGA hats and

command them to storm the Capitol," I said.

"And maybe kill his hapless sidekick Shady Vance," said Jackson."

As always, the prospect of impending injustice aroused my dormant inner priest. "And much, much more," I said.

Another long silence fell.

"So as American citizens who love our country," said Byrne, "the time has come to rid the Devil."

I shared a look with Jackson. Neither of us believed in witches and devils. But Byrne had piqued our curiosity. And an exploratory trip to Mar-a-Lago might create some other opportunity to thwart any Trumpian scheme to create yet another insurrection.

"My Fox contact might be able to arrange something," said Jackson.

Just two days later Byrne and I received a text from Jackson.

> Hi there, you guys. Seems a meeting of evangelical supporters has indeed been scheduled. My contact couldn't get me into it, but since you're both evangelicals—that's what I told him, anyway—he's arranged rooms for the two of you to stay at Mar-a-Lago for the night, grab dinner in the dining room, then in the morning participate in the meeting and figure out the best way forward with your work.
>
> As always I remain your obedient servant.
>
> Just saying.
>
> Jackson.
>
> PS: On the subject of good and bad behavior, I'm attaching another excerpt from my memoir on how trusted officials go off the rails.
>
> PPS: Margot and I are thinking of junketing to Palm Beach to spend a few days with a couple of friends, so our paths might still cross down there.

PART THREE

*"By the pricking of my thumbs
something wicked this way comes."*
Shakespeare, Macbeth

WHEELCHAIRS

Our schedules were such—Byrne's and mine—that we agreed to travel separately and meet up at Mar-a-Lago. I was on my way out my apartment door when I decided to duck back to my bedroom chest of drawers and pluck out the American flag lapel badge someone had given me, and pin it into my jacket buttonhole. Then I went downstairs and grabbed a cab to LaGuardia Airport. The check-in was fast, so, with time to kill, I pulled a printout of a PDF from Jackson's memoir. Happily he'd also included some comments...

Hi there, Paul. Per our conversation, I'm attaching some excerpts from my prison memoir. This first piece on the subject of the divine intervention will likely catch your interest.

How To Get Out Of A Wheelchair

Antz stepped gingerly to the front of the class. "The belief that got me into trouble was that friends would always look out for me. Nobody's asked me, but you've wondered how I got my limp, right? Well, I got this hop—and this bad back—'cos three so-called friends got pissed off over nothing, then beat me unconscious and tossed me off the top of a ten story building. They meant for me to die on the concrete path but I landed on a patch of lawn, which is why I'm still alive. It happened 12 years ago, when I was 28. I woke up in a hospital bed and stayed there for six months. Then I failed physical therapy. It was three months of hell. They sent me home in a wheelchair and said I'd never walk again." He paused, took a deep breath. "I was sitting in that wheelchair and staring at my bedroom wall. I was tight with fury at those fuckers. After a few months, I also got to thinking that I really did want to walk again. So you know what I did? I've never been religious, but I prayed to God. And you know what? A voice came out of the air. 'First you gotta forgive those guys who threw you off the roof' is what it said! I thought about that for a minute. Then I decided to forgive those guys. I said the words out loud and that was easy. But to try to step out of the wheelchair was hard. A wheelchair can be very comfortable. I sat there for what seemed like a lifetime. Then I grabbed my crutches and jerked myself up. It was torture, and I only managed three excruciating steps. But I knew it was a new beginning." He tossed a smile in my direction. "All things considered, even though I'm back in jail, I mighta been lucky to wind up in this class."

As something of a nonbeliever myself, I found Antz's story intriguing. I was still thinking about it after his release. I try to stay in touch with the guys who complete my class. What they say outside the prison walls can be pretty inspiring. Or sometimes not. I'll be keen to get your take on my follow-up meeting in the city with Antz...

Maybe Jackson was struggling to escape his own Socratic cave? If so, these guys were following him into the light. What to say? **"Boarding Now!"** Airport announcements always seem urgent. I'd have to read about Jackson's follow-up meeting with Antz later. I dropped the printout into my satchel and shuffled aboard where a new set of new life-lessons awaited...

FLIGHT LESSON

So here I was, Florida-bound in Business Class. A fellow traveller—balding, bearded, bland and sixtyish—removed his blue jacket, packed it into the overhead rack, and plumped his gray pants into the empty seat beside me. "I'm Russ," he flashed a grin, "but my friends call me Russell."

"And I'm Paul."

"On a journey to Damascus?"

"Kind of, maybe."

He eyed my flag-pin. "So have you figured who you going to vote for?"

It was a cheery question. I mulled a noncommittal answer.

"I'm still not sure."

"There's only one man in it... one real man... I mean Biden was weak as water and not all there."

"But he's resigned?"

"And Kamala's worse."

Trumpsters intrigue me. I could understand why one might vote for the orange fellow back in 2016. But why would anyone vote for a twice-impeached, thirty-four times convicted felon? I opened up what I hoped might be an enlightening chat. "I guess it all comes down to policy."

"You got that right! And she's a crazy, radical lefty liberal." He looked at me earnestly. "So why're you having a problem making up your mind?"

"Well, I'm looking at the low and falling inflation, four percent unemployment, and the Dow is over forty thousand."

"Oh no," he said, distressed at my naïveté. "No, no, no." He scuffed his Gucci loafers. "We can't trust *any* of those figures."

"Really?"

"Yeah. Whenever we're closing in an election they fake those stats. Then, afterwards, they go back to normal, which in Kamala's case"—he shot me a smile—"means disastrous."

So there it was. Denial. But I wasn't off the hook.

"And, as well as being weak,"—he dropped his voice to a stage whisper—"these people are, uh, *evil*. I mean just about everybody's saying it."

"Evil? Really? How so?"

"Well, for openers, on the abortion issue they're hypocrites. I mean, they should be opposed to murdering babies. But they champion ripping babies from a mother's womb, then executing them. And crazy Kamala approves."

"I guess they mistakenly believe in the separation of church and state."

"Right again. And the mistake is huge. I mean the Roe v Wade got overturned. The Supreme Court decided that, right?"

"With President Trump's help, of course."

"Yes, indeed."

"It's shameful he's a convicted felon."

"Everyone knows that New York trial was rigged. New York? *Sin City*. But God always finds a way."

I couldn't resist a pun. "So Trump might have penetrated the Storm..."

"*Divine intervention!* It's how Trump came to us. God spared him from an assassin's bullet. And how God appoints Judges and Justices. You know about divine intervention, right?"

"I'm a believer."

"So you know that divine intervention makes sense. God finds gifted sinners to do His work. It's written in the Good Book. He works in mysterious ways." He drew a deep breath. "You better believe it."

Divine intervention. Or maybe, as Byrne would say, Devilish Intercession. Either way it's a double-edged blade. But what about his take on abortion? To be fair, it's a tricky issue. The head says one thing, the heart another. For some it comes down to "murdering babies." For others, abortion should be "safe, legal, and rare"—and if there is to be a choice it should be the mother's, not black-robed theocrats. But wait a minute, Paul. If you're being honest you'll confess that if your own mother had been in a position to make an actual choice, you mightn't have ever got to breathe God's air. So maybe that was divine intervention. Or maybe just a Mother's Choice. No need to pontificate. Or get pulled in by this one-sided Floridian rant. But what always intrigues me is that we humans are given to certitude on so many issues. Oh, what the hell? Here endeth the lesson.

"Excuse me," I said, politely. "But I've got to catch up with some vital homework." It was still in my lap, so I unzipped my slim leather attache.

"You're a man on a mission." He waved his pink hand over the cabin. "But aren't we all?"

I nodded a smile.

As I riffed through my satchel I became conscious of my new-found friend peering at my fingers. First came the file I kept for Byrne's research papers. Atop that pile would be his piece, *How to Exorcise a Fiend.* Best not let my curious friend catch sight of that. I was looking for Jackson's follow-up conversation with Antz, when, I'm sure you'll understand why, a piece by Byrne caught my eye...

PARADOXICAL DENIAL BY VICTIMS OF EVIL

Victims of possession by the Devil might also engage in denial as a coping strategy. Facing the reality of being subjected to evil—whether through manipulation, abuse, or betrayal—can be profoundly disturbing and disorienting. Victims may deny the truth in an effort to maintain a sense of normalcy or to safeguard their emotional well-being.

Such denials can prevent victims from fully recognizing their situation, protecting themselves and seeking justice. There are also significant psychological and spiritual consequences.

Such encounters can lead to a deep crisis of faith or a destabilization of one's world view. Facing malevolence in another human being can challenge deeply held beliefs about reason, justice, and the inherent good in people. This confrontation is not just with the perpetrator but also an internal moral and spiritual struggle within the victim or the bystander.

So we need to see things as they really are without the cloud of denial. We need to engage in serious confrontation. Such conflicts should come from a desire for the truth, not just retribution. We need to be able to identify and name evil actions and tendencies, not merely in others, but within ourselves.

I glanced sideways. The beak of my fellow-passenger was buried inside the charcoal covers of a well-stuffed file. The Good Book was also within his reach. I continued foraging through my satchel files—and there it was…Jackson's follow-up conversation with the fellow whom God commanded to step out of his wheelchair…

Wheels within Wheels

Antz set his fork neatly down on his empty plate, and

dabbed his napkin to his lips. He'd arrived neatly turned out in a grey bomber jacket, black jeans, a tan collared shirt, and black slipons. I didn't much notice his limp, just that he was fit and poised—suave even—more so than I remembered. Someone not to be taken lightly, I thought.

"Things are going well now?" I asked.

"I'm still finding my path, but I'm doin' okay. I gotta minimum wage job but I'm moving in that direction 'cos the boss likes me,"—he grinned—"which is new for me."

"Hey, that's great." Should I ask the next question? Why not? "One other thing I was wondering. You said that you heard God's voice tell you that you could only get out of your wheelchair if you forgave the guys who threw you off the roof, right?"

"Yeah, that really happened."

"So what did that voice sound like, exactly?"

He paused and looked me in the eye. "That voice… well… it was as clear and as calm as you're sounding to me right now."

"Really."

"It really was."

"So what went down that made God so keen for you to forgive those guys?

"Well, listen,"—he glanced over his shoulder, then dropped his voice—"I was dealing then. The top floor of that building was empty, so we agreed to make the delivery there, then share a Friday night high. Three guys showed up with a girl and some blankets. They paid me, then spread their blankets on the floor and sat down and started right in on the product. I waited awhile, then decided not to hang around. It was a warm night, so I figured I'd be safest on the roof. I had some blankets of my own up there, actually. The girl climbed up with me and I locked the trapdoor behind us. We both got high, then we, uh, made love. Then we crashed, uh, nodded off." He took a deep breath. "But when the guys downstairs woke up and the girl was gone and the roof door was locked, they figured out where we were. They climbed the ladder, smashed open the trapdoor and grabbed their money out of my jacket. Then they picked me up by my arms and legs, wound up with a couple of swings and sent me flying off the roof." We sat in silence for maybe half a minute. "I guess they were pissed that I used their moolah to pay off their girl."

"Pay her off?"

"Yeah, well, she needed some drugs so I gave her some. And I slipped her some cash for, uh, taking care of me."

So, now Antz's story made sense. He took a handsome fee for supplying drugs to his friends, and then he whisked away their girl and fed her habit—and used their money to pay her to slake his carnal needs. No wonder, when they woke, that the so-called friends felt like victims. No wonder they clawed back both the money and the girl. No wonder that their wrathful, righteous inner demons unleashed full fury upon their malefactor. No wonder, before healing the apparent cripple, that God—or someplace inside Antz' brain—commanded him to forgive the so-called friends who effected his downfall. It had been a tragedy for all concerned. Fortunately nobody died, not that night anyway. Should I have spelled out that moral for him? I didn't think so. His tone and the glances we'd shared suggested that if he hadn't already, he'd make his own reckoning. Personally, I took comfort in pondering that Antz's God is wise and forgiving—and converses in plain English in a voice indistinguishable from my own.

It must be great to be infallible. Or even to be certain of just about anything. But that's not me. Even if we don't go ahead with this drastic, ancient, supposed sacrament—sometimes I can't even bring myself to say that 'E'-word—the mission of introducing light into the Trumpian organs might meet with some success. Most people don't realize that persuasion involves a process. Happily, I have some expertise in that, so I might just be able to work some magic. Meantime the humming of the plane was comforting and lulled into me a fitful sleep...

> *In my dream I was at a river, one of a thousand onlookers, observing the baptism of a blond headed orange teenager in a silken gown. The officiating minister was black robed Supreme Court Justice Clarence Thomas. Pressing the boy before him, Thomas waded up to his neck into the murky water. Then turned the boy face down, pressed him deep down into the water and held him there, until, finally the thrashing boy whirled to the surface. "I seen Jesus," he blubbered, "I seen Jesus, I seen Jesus, I seen Jesus." Thomas grabbed the orange blob by its throbbing shoulders. "No," he declared. "It was just a turtle." Then, pressing the struggling torso face down, he turned to the onlooking crowd and repeated the line. "It was just a turtle," he explained, "just a turtle... He continued to press the blob back down deep into the water, then held it there until ...*

"Time to wake up and smell the roses," said my bearded fellow passenger. And indeed, in aromatic Florida, there were multi-colored flowers and sunny delights for every taste. As I was soon enough to apprehend...

DEVIL'S GATE

I passed through the handsome, wrought-iron gates, sucked the sickly-sweet, humid air and saw for myself why *Mar-a-Lago* is Spanish for sea-to-lake. I stepped inside, pressed the door closed, and perhaps expecting a welcome note, glanced to the empty floor in front the brushed-brass mail slot. My room was, as expected, one of the smaller chambers, but nicely done in the style of the Floridian age gone by. A tiny window was tucked into a sky-wall. The queen-size bed was draped with a scarlet duvet. A two-person sofa sat alongside one wall. On the opposite wall a dark-oak bench sat in front of black high-backed chair. Given Trump's New York fraud conviction for lying about the value of his New York apartment, I checked the Mar-a-Lago history from a brochure laid out on the bench. The essence of what I learned was that...

> Mar-a-Lago was built in the 1920s on 17 acres of prime real estate, as winter home to socialite Marjorie Merriweather Post. She hired a designer and invested $123 million in current dollars. At that time it was the most expensive non-royal residence ever built. In 1969 it was designated a national historic site. Mr. Donald J. Trump, bought it as his private residence in 1985 for $7 million. In 1994, after the local council thwarted his attempt to sell it into smaller properties, he converted it into a members-only private club with guest rooms, and hotel-style amenities. In 1995 he gave up the right to use Mar-a-Lago other than as a social club, and signed a Deed of Conservation and Preservation. Then in 2002 he agreed to a conservation easement preventing further development.

> The Trump family maintains private quarters in a closed-off area on the grounds. Since 2019, for tax purposes, Trump has designated Mar-a-Lago as his primary residence. Effectively,all Mar-a-Lago is a private club for

members to enjoy between Halloween and Mother's Day. It also happens to include Trump's private and official residence, so he votes in Palm Beach County and pays no State income tax.

Architecturally, Mediterranean-style villa. The setup—a two-story central block with family quarters and service areas in lower subsidiary wings and buildings—was chosen by Mrs. Post to keep the main house from appearing too massive and to separate the family and service areas from those used for entertaining. The house has 58 bedrooms, 33 bathrooms, a 29-foot-long (8.8 m) pietra dura marble-top dining table, 12 fireplaces, and three bomb shelters.

It didn't take long to settle in, so, as you might imagine, I decided to take a walk and look over as much as I could of Mar-a-Lago. In fact, as I closed the door of my room behind me, I was halted in the corridor...

CHANCE MEETING

Bizarrely, to my mind anyway, Trump was standing in the marbled hall. As our eyes locked I got the feeling that perhaps he'd spotted a red light in the middle of my forehead. My surprise was leavened by the fact that I had heard rumors of other such so-called chance meetings with him. The buzz was that he was lonely, so new guests were a source of comfort, that he often lay in wait to engage. "Welcome to Mar-a-Lago," he beamed. The ear that had been grazed didn't rate even a Band-Aid. His smile was warm, empathetic, and disarming. I glanced over my shoulder to see whether he intended for someone else. But no. We were alone. At least for now. His warm demeanor was akin to that of a great old friend. Clearly, his words were addressed to me and me alone. "It's magnificent, right?" He raised and waved his hands in a circular motion. "It really is. Nothing like it anywhere in the world. I bought it in the eighties—or maybe God intervened and made me buy it. I mean, you heard about how I got saved and saved again, right?" I nodded. "Of course you have. Only consequential presidents are ever saved twice. Never forget that. and God chose for me to live at Mar-a-Lago, too. I've lived here ever since he chose me to buy it. I made it an exclusive club. Really exclusive. You see those marble dolphins over there, that's where my family lives." As he turned and waved he seemed to emit a curious fragrance. "The whole place is famous." He turned back to me. "Just about as famous as I am actually. For sure it's the most famous place in Palm Beach. Probably the most famous in Florida. We've had dinner parties, charity events, concerts, costume balls, international white-ties, tails, and tiara Red Cross galas. Even a circus. It's famous world over actually. Only Trump Tower might be more famous. Mar-a-Lago, it's a national historic landmark.

I guess everybody knows that." His breath was blended with peppermint. His hair and face were also perfumed with a funky combination of lacquer, aftershave, and suntan lotion. "The powers that be said it showcased the baronial way of life." He seemed to sense that I'd fallen into thinking about his whiff. It was as if the red light on my forehead had dimmed. Fixing me with both eyes he pursed his lips. "*Baronial!*" He emphasized the word then paused. Apparently satisfied that the red light was glowing again, he continued. "I guess these days I'm a Baron, too. Maybe you know that we—Melania and I—called our son, *Baron?* Baptized him actually. He's really smart you know. Really bright. Genius level, maybe. When you come to dinner you might meet him. I mean you *will* be dining here tonight? Of course you will. Never know who you'll meet. I've personally hosted Celine Dion and Billy Joel. You've heard of them, right? We've had beauty pageants too. I call it my Winter White House. But everybody's welcome. So long as they pony up the couple of hundred grand entry fee, of course. We all have to chip in and pay our fair share, right? And like I said, we accept everybody. Jews, Muslims, Indians, Asians, and Blacks of every shape, color and size. I mean, if you've got a couple of hundred grand to spare I could get you a membership. You'd be able to stay here. Like I do. I'm always here. Except when I'm campaigning. As I'm sure you know, all sorts of world leaders come to meet me. Melania has a big following, too. A huge following actually. When I opened the New York Plaza Hotel, one of the finest in the world—well it was when I owned it—I came up with a tagline, *Nothing Unimportant Ever Happens at the Plaza.* That took off as I'm sure you know. Everyone was saying it. They even talked about it in my *Time* magazine front cover Man of the Year profile—you heard about it, right? And there were many more *Time* cover stories, by the way, especially anyway, here at Mar-a-Lago since I became President and made America Great Again. We host all sorts of other world leaders, too. Like, uh, Shinz Abe—I liked him immensely—and, uh, Xi Jinping—a really great guy, I can tell you that for sure—and, uh, Jair Bolsonaro, who admired me greatly. They all did. I mean you've heard of these guys, right?" He dropped his voice to a conspiratorial whisper, "We also monitored the missile strike on Syria from our private SCIF... but you never heard that from me, right?" He played an invisible concertina with his curiously pale hands. "We've got Doria stone from Genoa and twenty thousand roofing tiles." Now his slim fingers pointed downwards. "And maybe five thousand black and white marble floor blocks from a castle in Cuba. And, and when you come to dinner tonight, you'll see a perfect example of the fifty thousand antique Spanish tiles we built into the entrance hall, patio, cloisters, and all the rooms. It's the largest collection in the world." He glanced to his Rolex. "And, in case things ever go wrong, we've got three bomb-shelters." His eyes darkened and a scowl crept into his orange face. "And so if that, uh, woman, that cackling, uh, female, that cackling, uh, black witch on a broomstick. I used to call her Cackling Kamabla. You know that, right? These days I call her Comrade Kamala." He shot me a wily grin. "She's a Marxist Communist and *everybody* needs to know it. And what about Sleepy Joe? What a pussy he turned out to be. People say he's lost it. In fact he's never been right in the head. But you know that, right? So now we have all Comrade Kamala. She's a bitch actually. Everybody knows that." His turn to rage was real enough. But clearly he remained in sales mode. I was to be his co-conspirator. Then, before Byrne might say Holy Toledo, he switched back again to warm and fuzzy mode. He smiled the widest of grins, then in one motion clasped my right hand with his, set his left hand on my shoulder, and held me in this almost wrestler-grip. "I'll be looking for you later, of course." Then he turned and ambled up the corridor and disappeared, leaving me with only that weird wafting scent.

Looking back, I liked the guy. Well, I guess I admired the sales persona he presented. It seemed authentic and sincere. And sad. The big-wide, braggadocio smile, the too-long handshake, the shoulder tapping, all of that. I guess that all his life he'd been exchanging this blend of charm and conspiratorial fury in the hope of winning a friend. He was the archetypal lonely guy doing whatever it took to seduce a client and make a sale. Well, anyway, that sales persona was doubtless merely one of his Russian nesting dolls. Maybe the last one might turn out to be Vladimir Putin. But even if that marketing mask enabled Trump to win the upcoming election, it would never be enough to sate his inner needs. To be fair, at the time of our 'chance' meeting, he probably believed every word he said. One way or another, however, it could never be enough, not for him. For sure, there were a raft of other dolls inside that outer casing. Or, as Byrne is always saying, the Devil hath power to assume a pleasing shape. I used to discount his theistic homilies. But I've learned never to disregard an intuition. So I went online, Googled *The Apprentice*, tracked down one of the early producers, and checked him out on LinkedIn. Luckily he'd left a phone number for the Press and potential new employers. And so I called. I'm chary of citing his name, but he was happy to take the call, and after a while I asked the question that had been troubling me. "Did you ever notice any kind of scent emanating from Mister Trump?"

A long pause followed. "Well, yes. What with the aftershave and orange cream and hair lacquer, there was always a smell about him."

"And body odor?"

"Well, yes again. He was obese so he was always sweating."

"And . . .

"We all noticed that from time to time he emitted a really bad smell. That's why in the show we seated him at the end of that lengthy boardroom table."

"And he never complained?"

"He was very happy to sit there. Seemed to give him comfort, actually. As long as he was in his boardroom seat he could do whatever he needed to do."

"Whatever he needed to do?"

"I'll be very honest. Most of our staff knew that Donald was, uh, incontinent. We just assumed he ate too many hamburgers. To be fair, he wore a diaper when he needed to let off steam. So on the sly we called him Diaper Don."

It can be difficult to discuss this kind of thing without smiling. But, to Byrne anyway, the question of who or what possessed Trump was serious indeed. On the basis of this conversation it surely seemed that on account of his fondness for chopped beefsteak Trump was merely incontinent. Or, perhaps, as Shakespeare noted about leaders who turn rotten, *sweetest things turn sourest by their deeds; lilies that fester smell far worse than weeds.* That might be something else to ponder.

ROAD AHEAD

We met in Byrne's room. Like mine it was small. The scarlet walls offset the brocade-sheathed queen-size bed. I stepped to the blue curtain adorning the single window that overlooked his view of the road and beyond that single-story, stucco habitats. "A comfortable Trumpian setup."

"God works in mysterious ways."

"Wheels within wheels."

"So it's all arranged. We'll break bread in the main dining room tonight. Then tomorrow morning we'll have two meetings in the Mar-a-Lago chapel."

"Mar-a-Lago has a chapel?"

"A Trump campaign setup for evangelicals. He also invites them to share the delights of the dining room."

"Clearly he respects their inner needs."

"A group of them will attend our first meeting. We'll anoint him with blessings and the laying on of hands, then offer appropriate prayers." He dropped his voice. "Unbeknown to them, our diabolist, will be part of the conclave."

"Then what?"

"They'll depart leaving the three of us with Trump. Then our man will introduce himself, and explain he's also there to drive out, uh, malignant spirits. Then he'll take over."

"Is he truly up for that?"

"Father Dunne has done hundreds of these sacraments. He'll work an actual miracle, you'll see."

"*Father* Dunne?"

"It won't matter that he's Roman Catholic. We'll have all sorts of religious leaders. And, God willing, the Reverend Franklin Graham. But, in his, uh, chosen calling, our man is in a league of his own. "

"From your lips to God's ears."

ANTICIPATIONS

When I got back to my room I closed the door, checked the lock, drew the curtain across the window, hung my jacket, lay on the bed, and opened and read the piece from Jackson....

As I recall, the last excerpt I shared from the prison memoir I'm working on was mostly drawn from denizens of the Rikers darkness. But, to quote an ancient poet, "Who will guard the guards?" So see what you think of this next extract...

As we passed through the C76 turnstiles Ashleigh pointed to a huge glass-encased black and white mural on a wall between a soda fountain and some payphones. "It's an original Salvador Dali," she said, "a Corpus Christi."

I checked the signature then studied the artefact. A floating black blob figure of Christ was impaled upon a heavy floating cross. I pondered the crown of thorns set amidst inky red-and-black splatters.

"It sure looks like a Dali."

"It originally hung in the cafeteria near the trash cans where the prisoners disposed of their leftovers. It racked up ketchup stains. In the eighties officials decided to clean it up and put it here. Dali had been booked to teach a Rikers art class, but he balked and created this instead. It arrived with a message from him to the prisoners. 'Life's not finished. You are artists. With art you're always free.'"

"So suffering leads to redemption, right?"

"That seems to be the idea."

***

Seven years later, after my class I headed for the Rikers parking lot. Hassan was waiting. Clasped inside his elbow was a folded copy of the Daily News. The day was grey but the city skyline was in full view. Our eyes searched the gaping hole in the New York skyline.

"Just not the same, is it?" he said.

"No. I stood on the corner of Fifth and Twenty-First

and watched the second Tower fall."

"And I saw it on TV." Hassan nodded sadly. "It was like a magician shot a bullet through those silver slabs. They puffed into the sky like a mushroom cloud. And when the smoke and mirrors cleared, they'd vanished."

"Yeah—it's not the same."

"The Salvador Dali got wiped out, too." He opened the paper. "Stolen by Rikers deputy wardens! Can you believe it?"

"Yeah, I heard it on the news. Got switched for a crummy counterfeit, right?"

"That's not the worst of it. One of those thieving idiot officials got scared someone would notice, so he burned the original"—he shot me a cynical look—"so he says."

"So, the Towers crumbled down"—we silently surveyed the scene—"and the Dali went up in flames."

Ah, Jackson. Perhaps he should've stuck to coaching corporate chiefs. Or maybe not. Given what was coming in the morning, I turned to Byrne's research paper on exorcisms...

Conference of Catholic Bishops on Exorcism

Final text of Exorcisms and Related Supplications, as confirmed by the Holy See in December 2016 and implemented in the dioceses of the United States as of June 29, 2017.

There are instances when a person needs to be protected against the power of the Devil or to be withdrawn from his spiritual dominion. At such times, the Church asks publicly and authoritatively in the name of Jesus Christ for this protection or liberation through the use of exorcism.

The solemn, or "major exorcism," a rite that can only be performed by a bishop or a priest, is directed "at the expulsion of demons or to the liberation [of a person] from demonic possession" (Catechism of the Catholic Church, no. 1673).

Only after a thorough examination including medical, psychological, and psychiatric testing might the person be referred to the exorcist for a final determination regarding demonic possession.

While all forms of exorcism are directed against the power of the Devil, the Rite of Major Exorcism is employed only when there is a case of genuine demonic possession, namely, when it is determined that the presence of the Devil is in the body of the possessed and the Devil is able to exercise dominion over that body.

The priest being appointed to the ministry of exorcism should possess piety, knowledge, prudence, and integrity of life.

If it is deemed useful, members of the lay faithful may be present for the rite, supporting the work of the exorcist by their prayers either recited privately or as instructed in the rite.

As part of the evaluation process, the afflicted member of the faithful should avail himself/herself of a thorough medical and psychological/psychiatric evaluation. Historically, however, the Church has exercised caution when evaluating such individuals for fear of unnecessarily drawing attention to the machinations of the Devil or giving credit where no credit is due.

Given the super-abundance of confusing and inaccurate information available in the public arena surrounding this topic, the manner in which this rite is announced provides for a teachable moment to believers and non-believers alike.

In addition to the use of the Psalms and Gospel readings and the recitation of the exorcistic prayers, a series of sacred symbols is utilized in the Rite of Major Exorcism.

To begin, water is blessed and sprinkled, recalling the centrality of the new life the afflicted person received in

Baptism and the ultimate defeat of the Devil through the salvific work of Jesus Christ. The imposition of hands, as well as the breathing on the person's face (exsufflation) by the exorcist, reaffirms the power of the Holy Spirit at work in the person as a result of his/her Baptism, confirming him/her as a temple of God. Finally, the Lord's Cross is shown to the afflicted person and the Sign of the Cross is made over him/her demonstrating the power of Christ over the Devil.

The norm is to celebrate the rite of exorcism in an oratory or other appropriate place (for example, a small chapel) discreetly hidden from plain view.

For the integrity of the afflicted person's reputation as well as for those individuals who might be assisting, the preservation of confidentiality is important. It is also strongly suggested that the identity of the exorcist be kept secret or at most known only to the other priests of the diocese so as not to overwhelm the exorcist with random calls and inquiries.

This reading reminded me why I welcomed becoming a failed priest. I prepared my morning clothes, and then disrobed, stepped into pajamas and quickly fell into a fitful sleep.

> *In my dream Satan was floating in front of the Pearly Gates. Three black-robed, straight-faced supplicants—Clarence Thomas, Samuel Alito, and Franklin Graham—ascended from the cloudy floor beneath him. Alito produced a scroll upon which six words glowed in a fiery font, The Truth Shall Set You Free. The Devil grinned and grabbed the scroll and waved them through the gates. Next to ascend were Jackson and Byrne and me. The Devil unfolded the scroll. This time it read Go Directly to Jail.*

I woke, stepped to the window, and gazed out. The sky was

clear but fading fast and a curiously pale twilight moon seemed on the rise. Whatever was I doing here? Maybe, as a failed priest, I was being pulled one way by the rationality of existential psychology, and another by supernatural forces of good and evil. Or maybe I was just a little moonstruck? There's a dark side and a light side to our inner lunar landscapes. The battle between good and bad behavior never ends. Happily, I'd soon know the outcome of this increasingly delicate and dangerous journey. I checked my watch. It was time to join the blessings of the assorted religious leaders. I slipped into my fresh white shirt and dark suit, knotted my red tie, and checked my mirror image. The flag-pin was a nice touch. I looked okay. I opened my door and, ready or not, stepped out into the battle for angels and devils and anyone else entrapped within the universe.

MAR-A-LAGO DINING

I'd heard that security was lax, so I wasn't unduly alarmed that no-one was checking credentials as I trekked to the Mar-a-Lago dining table and seated myself in my reserved place alongside Byrne. To my chagrin, he mellifluously announced, "Paul's here, praise the Lord." A chorus of "praise the Lord"seemed to follow. I don't exactly remember, but something in my brain may have sparked me to reply, "And joy to thee."

"Such a beautiful room," said a voice.

"Magnificent, indeed," said another.

To my admittedly jaundiced eye, the space was gaudy and overdone. But it strictly honored the integrity favored by Floridian nouveau riche. Bronze blue panels within golden walls. Three crystal chandeliers hung from scarlet circles studded into the fresco adorned ceiling. "And all of this, within our winter White House," said the Rabbi. Others were quick to chime in... "A truly special place"... "Everybody wants to visit"... "The most magical and holy place in America"... "The center of the universe."

Indeed, I thought, a Trumpian Xanadu, *a miracle of rare device / a sunny pleasure dome with caves of ice*. Hardly had I silently mouthed these words than Byrne nudged me. Trump had manifested at the dining room door. He tapped his ears, fluffed his blue suit, flicked his red tie to his groin, and primped to full height—and, or so I imagined, red lights in his followers' foreheads gleamed. The congregated diners stood, burst into worshipful applause and cries... "The greatest president in America's history... Praise the Lord... Our Savior has entered our lives..." And now their genuflections fell into a rhythmic chant. "U-S-A!... U-S-A!... U-S-A!"

Smiling broadly, Trump accepted their accolades, then,

as the chanting slowed, stepped to a waiting microphone. "I want to thank you all for your support." More applause. "And I hope everyone is enjoying the banquet because," he glanced back over his shoulder, "your ultra-busy first lady, Melania—who happens also to be my beautiful wife—made a special trip from New York's ultra-famous Trump Tower to be here tonight. Clad in a strapless black gown she stepped momentarily forward but remained eerily deadpan. As Melania likes to say, 'there's no place like Mar-a-Lago.'" He paused and beamed. "*Really!* There is simply no-place-on-this-planet—or any other—like Mar-a-Lago." More applause. "But I gotta tell you,"—he grinned—"Comrade Kamala is a crazy Marxist, and cognitively challenged Crooked Old Joe might recover from the coup she rigged"—he pointed his right finger to his left bicep—"but he could never hit a golf ball as far as I do."

He snatched Melania's hand, tightened his grip around her fingers, and led her and Eric and Don Junior and their wives to their round, rope-ringed center dining setting, an arm's-length from ours.

"I'm honored to be sitting so close to our President," said one of our evangelicals. In fact, Trump seemed oblivious to our presence. For sure, he'd forgotten his chance meeting with me.

Byrne's elbow prodded my ribs. "The club's menu has 'Mr. President's Wedge Salad,'" he said. "And I'm told the Mar-a-Lago hamburger buns come emblazoned with his likeness."

I felt a tap on my shoulder. "Excuse me." It was a Muslim cleric. "But I absolutely must ask Mister President to share his advice on a matter of extreme importance to my community." The Rabbi leaned forward. "God willing, he will permit any question." He nodded to me. "Mister President is widely noted for generously sharing his wisdom with truth-seekers."

Indeed. So long as Trump can imagine a camera and a red light in a supplicants forehead gleaming back at him, the Mar-a-Lago borders are porous for paying patrons. And foreign nationals, madmen, bad actors, or whatever are welcome in the private club Mister President calls his home. Kooks could get his advice on anything from national security to domestic policy, then share it with other kooks or causes.

"It sure beats sitting in a criminal courtroom trial," I whispered to Byrne.

"There's a strict dress code, but some guests seem not to know which fork to use." He glanced down. "Watch out!' he whispered. "He's heading our way."

Indeed, here was Trump, leaning across our table, his lips drawn into his widest smile. "I just need to thank you all in God's name—and, uh, in the name of Jesus, and, uh, Mohammed, and all of our sacred leaders—for your investment in, uh, breaking bread with your, uh, divinely spared President." If if recent events had doused his optimism, he didn't show it. He'd clearly showered, cleaned himself up, lacquered his comb-over, and pulled on a freshly dry-cleaned blue suit. But again, I nosed a curious aroma. Trump cast a fulsome smile over our table's guests, but seemed not to recognize any one. "As you know"—his tone had abruptly changed—"the last election was *rigged*. And the Justice Department has been *weaponized* against me. But I'm still the legitimate President of the United States of America." He paused. "And never forget,"—I sensed the line that was coming— "only consequential presidents are spared twice." He primped and bathed in the applause. "Praise the Lord," chimed evangelical voices. An echo of others followed. "Chosen by the Lord himself." Melania's Sphinx-like face peered out from behind Donald. Her wide, dark eyes seemed to settle on mine. It seemed a purposeful glance. Did she know who I was? What might she want? But then, like snow upon the pyramids, her glacial countenance vanished, and apparently wrapped within a coterie of security agents, she quietly departed the room.

Donald, unaware of her cameo or departure, went right on with his message. "I am fighting the good fight for all of you. The chimers rang again. "And you will win!"... "For God is on your side..." He smiled. "That crazy, rabid New York prosecutor Alvin Bragg—Fat Al is what I call him—is one hundred-and-ten percent corrupt. So is his federal judge. You all know that. The Supreme Court knows it too. That's why they're on our side." A voice cried, "Praise the Lord." Then someone broke into song. *"This train don't carry no gamblers..."* Others joined in. *"We're all on board the righteous and the holy."*

Mister President's chest swelled and his wide smile shone. "Thank you, thank you, thank you. But now if you'll excuse me, I have work to do. Important work. *Very* important work." He nodded and an assistant handed him an iPad. "So let me think a moment," he said. "Yes, of course." He'd assumed the role of disc jockey. An admiring follower stage-whispered, "Some nights Mister President chooses a spiritual medley, or something from *The Phantom of the Opera*." Trump tapped the iPad. "Tonight, for our special guests at this table, I shall play *"How Great Thou Art,"* by the ultra-famous Mormon Tabernacle Choir." We touched our hands to our hearts. Mister President continued tapping at his iPad. "Hmm... don't seem to have it here right now... But never mind. This might be better, anyway. Ladies and gentlemen, let's hear for... *The Village People!"* He cocked his wrists, set them to undulating, and mouthed their famous line as it boomed from the public address system,—'You better stay at the Y.M.C.A.' The congregation shuffled to their feet, and followed the rhythms and lip-synched vocals of the leader of the free world. And then that same curious aroma, but staler than before, seemed to be coming in waves that matched his rhythm. I might have been the only person who noticed, but, perhaps noting Melania's absence, with a low-key wave to his guests, Trump gave quietly exited the room.

We met in Byrne's suite. He gently closed the door, checked the lock, and turned. "Intriguing, right?" His tone was hushed.

"The red light never dimmed."

"He melts if it does," I said.

"Like the Wicked Witch from the West?"

"His advisers are telling him to forget the insults and nicknames, and lay out some serious policy differences."

"He never stays on script."

"And never will. He's a performer, and policy wonk is a role beyond his skills. But no matter. His fans go to hear an entertainer not an educator. So he plays the hate-filled comedy rant and they applaud."

"And the red light stays on?"

"That's the deal." I stepped to the door. "It's been a long day." Byrne's eyes locked on mine as he released the lock. I gave him a long hug. I tried to think of something to say, but no words came to me. We shared a look.

"Father Dunne will do us proud," he said.

In my dream, a gorilla was dancing on a marshy reserve and leading a line of children dressed in rags towards an alluring black-robed woman carrying a mandolin. Standing her ground she struck a vibrant chord. Then accompanying herself began to sing. The ragged children gathered around her robes with upturned faces. The gorilla began to sink, as if into the quicksand.

BLESSINGS

I didn't need an alarm clock to wake me in time to attend the blessings and the exorcism. I brewed a coffee and grabbed a croissant from the minibar. After quaffing those, I slipped into my dark suit, fresh white shirt, black slip-ons, and slipped my already knotted red tie over my head and carefully adjusted it. Who, really, is that flag-pinned actor within the mercury image? What's happening in his heart? Will good triumph over evil? I would know in mere moments. And I was wrong about everything.

A sky-blue door, gold-lettered 'Private' opened off the hallway into a modest vestibule where an assistant behind a counter passed each of us a small numbered plastic circle in exchange for whatever we didn't care to carry. At the press of a button on a security panel beside her, a second blue door slid open for communicants to enter or depart the chapel itself. Once inside, three light-oak pews surrounded an open space facing, one step higher with a two step apron, a modest altar bearing a white silk dressing and two glowing, presumably electricity-driven candles inside golden candlesticks. Above the altar, to my eye anyway, a life-size crucifix would normally hang. Today, that space was hung with what seemed an almost abstract, multicolored non-denominational religious tapestry, beneath which, threaded large enough to read, was the Latin phrase, *In Deo Speramus.* Sure, In God We Trust. The lighting was subtle and indirect. The glossy floor beneath our feet was shellacked, whitened timber planking.

As the sliding door opened and closed, I silently counted eleven participants as they arrived and gathered in clusters on the glossy floor between the altar and the pews. Apart from a Rabbi and a kaftaned Muslim cleric, the conclave seemed mostly pale and Christian. Father Dunne was shorter than most, a little on the pudgy side, and, in his black suit and shirt and priestly starched-white collar, almost indiscernible. He briefly nodded in our direction, then faded back into the gathering. "I see no trace of the Reverend Franklin Graham," whispered Byrne. He nodded towards the bearded Rabbi: "He's a regular on Fox." Byrne paused. "And I'm pretty sure the guy he's talking to is the big shot with the 2025 plan." I glanced in their direction. Oh no! The Rabbi seemed okay but that other ingratiating face belonged to my fellow-traveler. He'd added a red tie, but the newly pressed garb comprised the same blue jacket and gray pants. He held my glance, momentarily puzzled, but seeming not to recognize me, moseyed to an evangelical friend.

The murmuring faded as, again, the sliding door opened.

But what was this?

It could not be, surely.

But, yes it was.

Two videographers entered the chapel walking slowly backwards while peering through their viewfinders back at the entrance portal. Next, with a somewhat out-of-kilter, grim expression, came silk-robed Reverend Franklin Graham.

Then, grasping a brown, faux-leather Bible, and pretending not to notice the cameramen, Trump clumped through the threshold.

Nobody else seemed to notice, but the sinner whom God had chosen—and saved from a speeding bullet—seemed to emit that same indelicate aroma I'd scented in our chance meeting. Trailing behind him came a thin and thirtyish, oily and balding, white-faced and dark-eyed Goebbels lookalike. Like scarlet cardinals seeking proximity to a Pope, a gaggle of the faithful gathered around Trump. Now came an unexpected turn. The Reverend Franklin Graham looked on with a wide, ambivalent smile as Trump passed his Bible to the bearded Rabbi, upon whom one of the cinematographers now focused. With an eye on the gleaming red light atop the camera, Trump said, "a gift for you, my, uh, holy, uh, friend."

The freckled, olive fingers of the Rabbi gingerly accepted the tome. "*Todah, Todah.* Thank you. Thank you," he said. "*Y'varechecha Adonai v'yishmerecha.* And may God bless you and keep you, Mister President."

As the cameras continued to roll, the Goebbels doppelganger jumped forward, touched the lapel of Trump's suit, glanced backwards and offered a command. "Now hear, O Lord, in honor of the fighting spirit of our President, the holy words of Reverend Franklin Graham."

Aligning himself behind the dark-oak lectern, the man of God raised his open palms aloft, allowed his eyes to linger upon each of us, then shared an introduction. "Experiences can change us... As all the world now knows, when President Trump was felled by an assassin's bullet, he rose again... rose with his fist raised, showing America his unshakable resolve to fight for our nation. I have always known President Trump to be a man of his word. I was with him at the United Nations when—as the first president in the American history to do so—he advocated for religious liberty worldwide. I know that as our forty-seventh president, he will keep his word to the American people to make America great again. So, gather around him, and let us pray...

> Our Heavenly Father, we come before you with grateful hearts. Thank you for saving the life of President Donald J. Trump. You have blessed this country more than any. Sadly, as a nation we have forgotten who was responsible for all the freedoms, liberties, and bounty we enjoy. So we pray for the fighting spirit of President Trump. Spare him from the evil forces of a weaponized Justice Department and give him the ongoing vision to secure

the future of this nation, and continue to protect him from his enemies. Surround him with advisers who offer sound counsel as we make America great again. Bring us together as one nation under God, indivisible, with justice and freedom for all. We pray for these thy favors, in the mighty name of my Lord and Savior, Jesus Christ, the King of Kings and the Lord of lords. *Amen.*"

Clutching his own brown Bible, Trump drew a breath. "I accept that blessing, Reverend Graham. I know in my heart that I deserve it... that we all deserve it... And that we all need to, uh,"—he glanced to a cue card—"gird our loins to fight for what is right in our holy war." His hands wafted back and forth. "So I shall join you in praying for an outcome in this election that justifies the brilliance—some say the sheer genius—that I have always brought to bear in my, uh, mission to," he pumped his fist, "Make America Great Again... and, uh, of course, to, uh, lead the world in peace."

Goebbels jumped forward, pressed his palm to Trump's lapel, and glanced backwards. "So let us all salute the fighting spirit of our one true President." Trump clutched his pink fingers to the baleful red tie draped across his groin as the full gathering, including myself and Byrne, laid our hands upon the Trumpian jacket.

"In Your image, God," intoned the Rabbi, "I and these stewards dedicated to justice now bless the courage of this devoted leader who possesses the foresight, and imagination to solve, as he did in the past, the threats to our future."

"God of history"—I recognized that unctuous voice as belonging to my fellow-traveler—"in your name we anoint the fighting spirit of President Donald J. Trump and beg you now to spare him from the infamy of weaponized justice, and ensure that he champions retribution for past indignities and makes America great again."

The kaftaned cleric's voice was mellow. "In the Name of Allah, the most gracious, the most merciful, we invoke Allah for leaders to enjoin the valiant struggle of President Trump in his fight to lead his people into righteousness, and, as he did before, remedy the problems bedeviling our country."

Then, after the merest twinkle of a glance to me, Byrne spoke up. "In the name of all that is holy, we call for your divine intervention to ensure that Donald J. Trump accepts his challenges with insight, and dedication, and burnishes America's status as a shining city on a hill."

Goebbels goose-stepped forward, "And that's a wrap," he said. He glanced to his Rolex. "Yes, indeed. We have more footage than we need for these upcoming fund-raising videos." He nodded to the videographers. "So the Gefährten, uh, you guys can leave." He checked himself. "First though"—he thrust out his left hand— "deliver the videos you shot." He half-smiled to Trump as his right hand patted a prominent bulge in his armpit. After delivering their files into his palm, Goebbels shepherded the videographers as they lugged their apparatus out the door.

Trump stepped out of the circle and addressed the gathering. "I'll be staying here awhile," he said. "As I'm sure you understand, a highly important matter calls for my opinion, uh, my advice, my counsel—my *recommendation*." He smiled. "So Melania has arranged a special table in the dining room for you guys, uh, our, uh, VIP guests, our divine advisors actually"—he pointed both forefingers in their direction—"and so, God willing, I'll be breaking bread there later." The sliding door opened, and, murmuring wise words among themselves, the Reverend Franklin Graham led them out of the chapel.

So, here we were then, Trump, Byrne, and me. And now, like a hitherto unnoticed leprechaun in a shady garden, Father Dunne stepped into the light...

EXORCIZING THE DONALD

I had a bad feeling. Clearly, Trump saw no need to engage in any psycho-therapeutic process. So, how, exactly, would we get to the so-called sacrament of the exorcism itself? And even in the unlikely event that Father Dunne succeeded in breaching the flaming denials of Donald Trump, how might his inner Lucifer react? Yes, in my pastoral work I'd heard confessions of noxious behavior. But this experience would be different. This time, according to Byrne anyway, we'd come face-to-face with the nesting Devil inside Donald.

I stepped forward. "Once again, it is such an honor to share time with you, Mister President." He looked at me blankly, as if we'd never met. He'd clearly forgotten our meeting. He didn't even seem to realize that mere minutes ago I'd laid my hand on his lapel and blessed him. Maybe he'd gotten so used to being a figure of worship that he felt no need to remember the face of any everyday supplicant. Or maybe all those prayers and laying on of hands had been for him, as surely as it was for me, an out-of-body experience. Or maybe I'd uncovered another nesting doll. Or maybe he truly was in cognitive decline.

"A great honour to be in your chosen and twice-spared presence, Mister President," said Byrne.

"In fact," said Trump, "for both of us it's more than just an honor to be in my presence. As you probably know, as the entire world knows, actually, I got saved by, uh, divine intervention... God himself saved me from *two* wicked assassination attempts." Taking care not to lose Byrne's attention, he glanced my way. "Just one moment... one *tiny* moment *before* the first shot happened—a hundredth of a second, or maybe even less, a thousandth maybe—God, or maybe it was Jesus, told me to turn my head. Being a lifelong

Christian myself, I heard the call." He seemed to be reliving the experience. "Then a bunch of silver bullets came whizzing, uh, faster than a speeding bullet, you've heard that line before, right? But this time it wasn't just a line. This time it was all real." Byrne was paying close attention. "I knew it then and I know it now because blood came gushing from my ear. Everybody knew it actually. I mean you've seen the television coverage, right? So what did I do? Everyone knows the answer to that. First, I fell—and then I rose... and then I held my fist above my head"— he replayed the circling fist bump—"and I said, as all the world knows—and if anyone doesn't it's all over television—I shook my fist and I commanded my followers to Fight and Fight and Fight!"

"Yes, fight the good fight," said Byrne.

Trump blinked. "Then God intervened *again.* He spared me from another bullet. So never forget," here came that line again, "God only spares consequential Presidents two times, uh, *twice.*"

"Perhaps his greatest blessing," said Byrne. He pointed in the direction of his now not so invisible cohort. "My special colleague, Father Dunne also shares your passion to fight the good fight." The priest stepped forward as softly as a fox.

"*Father* Dunne. Roman Catholic, right?"

"Indeed, I am." He took a step back and up onto the altar apron. Now, with Trump a tad beneath his gaze, the diabolist seemed almost to uncoil into a taller, trimmer, stronger force.

"So, on the, uh, abortion policy," Trump shone a sales-mode smile, "I'm guessing you approve of the way that I got the Supreme Court to push that killing babies issue, uh, that, uh, troublesome social problem, off the table, uh, back to the States. I mean it's a States' rights issue, uh, thing, for them to deal with, right?"

The diabolist nodded sagely and took a deep breath. "I

would like to share the deeper dimensions of our communal divinity"—his Irish brogue was gentle—"and, most especially, into the heart and soul of the most powerful person in the world, being, as we all know, your esteemed and holy self, Mister President." Trump beamed. It seemed a happy omen. "I gather that as a lifelong Christian you have always been guided by what we Catholics believe to be the Holy Spirit?" In affirmation, as if preparing to pray, Trump clasped and squeezed his hands together. "And that you shy from what modern psychologists call the light of psychotherapy." Trump raised and squeezed his right fist. "It's mumbo-jumbo for weaklings," he said. "If there was any truth in it we wouldn't wind up with idiots like Crazy Nancy and Comrade Kamala." He held the diabolist's steady gaze. "So I never have and never will let any shrink mess inside my, uh, my God-given brain."

"So you believe in the spiritual world?"

"All change comes from God," said Trump. "And He chose me, then chose me again, and again, and again for all I know, to make America great again."

The diabolist remained impassive. "So I shall call upon these gifts from Pope John himself,"—I might have been seeing things, but Trump seems to jitter as Father Dunne raised a timeworn, leather-bound, gilt-edged, black tome and an ancient bronze crucifix into the air—"and ask you, Mister President, to follow me in the words of the one hundred and nineteenth psalm.

"The Lord is my refuge."

Trump blinked. Would he comply? Yes… in his fashion.

"The Lord is in my corner,"

"And I will make the Most High in your dwelling, O Lord."

"And I will make the most of the Most High, O Lord."

"So with your protection no harm will overtake me, and no disaster will come near my dwelling."

"So with your protection no disaster will ever come near me or my beautiful Mar-a-Lago home."

Father Dunne stretched his priestly starched collar and indicated that he alone would recite these next lines... "*For He will command his angels to guard you, and they will lift you up in their hands, so that you will not strike your foot against a stone... and you will tread on the lion and the cobra and trample the great lion and the serpent—*"

"I'll tread on lions and snakes?!" Might Trump have sensed where all this might be leading? "Like that snake with the AK forty-seven who tried to bring me down? But then I rose again, right?" Trump seemed not have twigged to Father Dunne's intention. Perhaps intuiting the initial disquiet of his subject, the diabolist slowed his delivery. "*So that our one true President, Donald J. Trump, may continue to make America great again... To which end, I call upon Jesus of Nazareth to drive out the demon.*"

As my brain silently replayed that last line, *To which end, I call upon Jesus of Nazareth to drive out the demon*, Trump's eyes seemed to glow, and an incongruous knowing grin seemed to break across his lips. And then, as if preparing to lift a heavy barbell, Trump clenched both fists and raised them to his shoulders. Then he moaned as he hefted this imaginary—or perhaps invisible?—burden and cried, "*Yes! Mama! Yes!*" The diabolist continued in his priestly brogue. "*Carry our prayers up to God's throne that the mercy of the Lord may quickly come and lay hold of the beast, the serpent of old, Satan and his demons,*"

Trump groaned as with apparently great effort he slowly raised the bar and again cried out, "*Yes! Mama! Yes!*"He showed that bizarre, knowing grin again, and lowered the unseeable barbell back to his shoulders.

"*casting him in chains into the abyss so that he can no longer seduce the nations.*"

Trump's eyes narrowed. "*Holy Shit!*" He glowered at the priest then cocked himself sideward. "*Jesus Christ!*"—he cried the name as if he were the victim of a flyby shooting—"*it's another fucking Witch Hunt!*" Upon those words the entire chapel became as black as night. A hissing seemed to follow and the weird smell seemed to rise into my nostrils. I may well have imagined hearing Trump cry again, "*Oh Mama, Yes! Yes! Yes!*" And now, or so it seemed to me, a sulfurous odor suffused the darkness. I may have been dreaming, but I thought I heard a buzz, and for sure I saw a flashing light. I blinked, and then, or so it seemed, hanging in the pungent air, I spied a ghastly, ghostly disembodied pair of flame rimmed eyes. And in that moment I also thought I heard the floor thump. A loud click followed, fluorescent lighting flooded the room, and I stared into the eyes of Goebbels. "The security of the President is my paramount concern"—his glottal voice was calm and cool—"so I never left the vestibule." He smoothed the bulge in his vest pocket glanced over the room. The candlesticks were overturned and the altar drapes were wildly askew or gone. And Trump had vanished. My eyes followed Goebbels' downward gaze. Father Dunne, his fist clutching the altar silk, was lying face down on the floor. Goebbels knelt and touched the priestly black suit. "Seems your friend might have suffered a heart attack," he said. "We can't leave him here. So you will leave and I will take care of things."

I tried to make sense of all this. What in the name of hell had happened? Had I attended a deadly game where Lucifer played the winning hand? Or, as some might suggest, had Trump himself, after having gorged himself on stale hamburgers, merely released himself into an already overburdened diaper. For sure, that would explain the hellish stench. But what about the barbell charade? Perhaps the pumping and groaning was just regression. Maybe he was reliving the pleasure an infant might share from his mother's smile as he released his gift into a chamber pot? If so, perhaps Goebbels failed to leave the chapel because he truly was concerned for the security of the President. Hence the bulge inside the armpit of his suit. Maybe it was a stun-gun? Might that explain the weird flashing in the blackness? Might is also explain the untimely passing of our diabolist? Was this the cue for me to choose between the complex forces of the Devil, and the perhaps simpler forces of human nature? It was something to ponder. It was a mystery. It was to me, anyway.

Byrne and I strolled out of the breakfast dining room into a quiet corner of the main lobby. He pretended to be calm and I kept my voice to a whisper. "I don't know how you feel," I said, "but we seem to have strayed into a devil's playground."

"No, no, no! We were in Satan's actual presence. You surely saw his fiery eyes, his knowing smirk, his bubbling skin, and we both inhaled the stench of his sulfur. We truly *were* inside the Devil's playground." He picked up on my silent uncertainty. "Yes, yes. Trump himself looked much the same as ever. But that's because he's still possessed. That's why, in our meeting with the religious leaders, his Inner Devil behaved as if nothing happened and now is off and about his evil business. But Father Dunne seems gone for good and the fellow you call Goebbels hasn't shown his face either."

Byrne is sure in his beliefs, of course. That's why he joined the church and became a cleric. But as my friends mostly know, I don't believe in supernatural forces, especially those imagined to bear a label of the Devil. Byrne likes to be taken seriously in serious discussions so I hope I hid my skepticism. "It is a cocoon of privilege," I said. "Outside these compound walls Trump is mostly ridiculed. But Mar-a-Lago is his castle."

"His safe zone?"

"Somewhere for a miscreant to hide from threats to reputation, wallet, and freedom. SCOTUS toadies may still yet try to help him win the November election."

"Even so, if the New York Hush-Money sentencing proceeds it will be hard to, uh, upend."

"Right now, Trump controls his so-called winter White House, straightens the pictures on the walls, and selects golden bathroom faucets.

"It truly is the Devil's safe zone," said Byrne.

"Last night I caught a fleeting glance of Melania."

"The Devil's handmaiden."

"You believe that?"

"I read somewhere that three years are missing from her life. Her early twenties, actually."

"Three years are unaccounted for?"

"As if she'd disappeared back to another planet."

"I'm sure she has a checkered history. Maybe she was being groomed by some fancy European escort agency?"

"Or whatever." Byrne raised his forefinger. "For sure she didn't truly qualify for the genius immigration status that Trump arranged. I mean have you studied her signature? It's there for all to see on Wikipedia. And the broadbrush, upright strokes are in exactly the same hand as that of her devilish husband." He sighed. "Oh, Paul! You still don't get it. Just look at what's happened. Father Dunne is lost and gone. Trump remains in full flight. His dodgy memory is devilish indeed. Lucifer obliterates events and people that need to be forgotten. He can be charming, but when the time is right his tongue turns to fire, and spits hate upon honest souls he perceives to be enemies."

"That's what you truly think?" I said

A rueful veil glazed his face. "I'm certain of it, actually."

Ah, yes, the certainty of faith. Yet again I have to

confess that with the passing of time, I've become plagued with doubts. *Lord I believe, help thou my unbelief?* Yes, yes. The wise are full of doubts. Qualms are disturbing but certainty seems absurd.

My cell phone vibrated. I don't usually answer unlisted calls, but this might be important.

"Is this Paul?" It was a halting mid-European female voice.

"Yes, I am Paul. How might I help?"

"We just a delivered a package to your suite. You have no doorman so we slipped into the mail slot in the door. I need to be sure that you are the person who collects it."

I'd glimpsed but only ever heard Melania on a CNN interview. "And who are We?"

"We is I... It is a gift."

"A gift?"

"You will know."

"And who are you?" I sensed that she was still on the line, but she made no attempt to answer my question. "A gift from whom?"

"You will know." She ended the call.

"You look worried," said Byrne. "Who was it?"

"I need to run back to my room," I said.

"So I'll meet you back in mine," he said.

I raced to my oak door and inserted my plastic key. Yes, it opened. And yes, a small, slim, cushioned manila envelope addressed to me lay beneath the mail slot. Was Goebbels sending me anthrax? I squeezed the envelope. Something hard was inside. It felt like a key. I figured that it was probably not a gift from Goebbels. I gently closed my door, and holding the envelope gingerly, stepped to my bed and, using my old-fashioned paper knife, carefully sliced open the package. There was no note. Just a monogrammed Mar-a-Lago USB stick. So long as the data was compatible with my iPad I could show it right now. But Byrne's room might be safer.

I stepped out into the corridor and was met by a uniformed fortyish, sallow-faced maid. She pointed back a few yards to a trolley. Her voice was calm and cultured. "I just need to top up your minibar," she said. Her unexpected presence was alarming. But I had the manila envelope and my iPad in my satchel, so I was leaving nothing of any value in my room. "No problem," I said. I paused a moment, then headed back to Byrne's room.

His eye was at the peephole. He unlocked and opened the portal, and as I stepped inside, gently closed and relocked it. The room, like mine, was small. And the single tiny window gave little light. I glanced around then dropped my voice. "I might have something we can share." I pulled the envelope and the iPad from my satchel. "Nothing special," I said.

He gave me a look as if to ask why I seemed to be whispering. I drew the USB stick from the envelope and held it aloft. "A gift from a friend," I said.

We sat on the side of his bed and loaded the stick into my iPad. There was just one item, a video. As I was about to open it, there was a knock on the door. Byrne stepped to the peephole. "It's the maid to check the minibar." He parted the portal. "Thanks, but a refill won't be necessary." She shared a professional smile with Byrne while eyeing me over his shoulder and glancing to the USB stick poking from my iPad. Byrne gave a nod, then closed the door. "I don't know what to make of that," I said. He sat back on the side of the bed and shared a smile. "Oh, Paul, you're so on edge!" Maybe so. I opened the video.

MONOCHROME PLEASURES

There was no sound-track. It was a monochrome of a young man, thirtyish or so, apparently engaging in carnal congress—I froze the frame—with no less than three beautiful, naked, alabaster-complexioned, teenage nymphs. Who was the lucky fellow on all fours — I unfroze the frame—pumping one nymph while fondling the breasts of another and being tongued from behind? Yes indeed. Donald. These acts of love soon ended. But then, the spruce and pale-fleshed fellow stood, and while swaying on the bed, doused his giggling threesome with a stream of yellow urine.

"Wherever," said Byrne in a whisper, "did you get this video?" I merely nodded and pointed to my iPad. Another video, this time in full color, had appeared. This time the action was in a grand and spacious room with huge four-poster bed. This time the chortling chap was decades older and obese. And this time a happy new threesome of gloriously young nymphs was giggling alongside him. Curiously, a thin smile was on his orange face, but his fulsome flesh was as white as the pure silk sheets into which he arced his golden shower. And then, this could not surely be, he spread his legs and sighed as slivers of beige faeces dropped upon the silk. "What the hell?" I whispered. Byrne shared a knowing nod. "He's deliberately defiling the bed Barrack and Michelle slept in when they were guests of the Kremlin." Yes of course. "It was all Trump could do at the time," I said. "But to be fair, as our forty-fifth president he made sure do the same to most every Obama achievement."

Byrne shook his head from side to side. "Here endeth the mystery of why Mister President is so obsequious to Putin. Always wise to the ways of libidinous young entrepreneurs, the KGB chief has been grooming him from the start."

"Indeed. And giving the green light to Donald's Russian Beauty Pageant was the master stroke of a master spy."

"He's often boasted Russia has the world's most beautiful, uh, ladies of the night."

"He knew that Donald would not resist these sirens."

"And so, at the very outset, on his first visit to Russia, Putin included carnal delights in the minibar."

"An altogether too-tempting *free-now, pay-later* program."

Byrne suddenly fixed an urgent gaze to the door. "Whatever is that sound?"

Byrne stepped to the peephole. "The wolf is at the door," he whispered. "Whatever will we do?"

"What *can* we do?" I slipped the iPad to the bedside table. "He knows we're here, so let him in."

It was indeed the dark-eyed Goebbels look-alike. He scanned the room then goose-stepped to the bedside table. "Ah yes," he said. He snatched the USB stick from my ipad and held it up. "Is monogrammed, you see, *Mar-a-Lago*." He smiled. "So stays mit us." He gently pressed it into his vest pocket. His voice turned somber. "Father Dunne passed in the night." I nodded but did not answer. "All things considered, we think it would be best for you and your, uh, comrade, to depart back to New York as soon as possible." He did not click his heels as I thought he might. "We can accommodate you on a private flight that we have leaving within the next few hours."

GETAWAY

Several cabs were waiting outside the Mar-a-Lago gates. Suspecting a Goebbels setup, we shared a glance. Then my iPhone vibrated. It was a call from Jackson.

"How did it all go?" he asked.

"All very successful," I said, cagily. "Will tell you all about it when we get back to New York. We're just leaving Mar-a-Lago and heading to the airport, actually."

"Great! Margot and I will meet you there."

"*You're* in Palm Beach?"

"We visited a couple of friends, remember?"

"And you guys are heading back now?"

"Our flight got delayed by a few hours—"

"—so we're stuck in the airport lounge," said Margot.

Byrne and I packed into the second-to-last of the waiting cabs and stayed silent on the ride to the airport. As we entered, a Barbie doll announced a FOX Breaking News headline:

An immigrant posing as a security agent threatened shoot vice-presidential candidate J.D. Vance as he was about to deliver a speech in Springfield, Ohio. Doctor Vance was unharmed, but the gunman has escaped and is at large.

"The Devil looking after his own?"

"Or maybe Trump planned it to foment the blood bath he's been promising—"

"—and keep the red light blinking—"

"—and appoint himself President—"

"—and stay out of jail."

Out of the corner of my eye, I spied what seemed to be Goebbels. As that fellow caught my glance, he faded back into the crowd. If it truly was Goebbels, my hunch is that he waited until we boarded our flight, and headed to New York.

FADING FORTUNE

Byrne sounded more than a little outraged. "Vance just said that a lie is just another way of telling the truth! He's defending Trump's lie about Haitians eating pets by saying Springfield constituents told him they'd seen something. So, as United States senator he's saying he was driven by noblesse oblige to share the truth by inventing what he calls a *story*." He drew a long sigh. "He really is a clever devil."

"He also spent a lot of time talking about a crime committed by an undocumented person in a state where Republicans have tried to make a campaign issue of violent immigrant crime," I said.

"In fact, immigrants have a lower crime rate people born here," said Byrne.

"Now, even more than Trump himself," I said, "Vance's eyes seem focused on the prize."

"The prize?"

"The prize for Vance is to become a Big-Shot, team up with his Svengalian mentor Peter Thiel, and implement Project 2025, whereas Trump is increasingly desperate to stay in a jail." I paused. "So he's likely to do something to upend the election before the results are in."

Byrne's eyes widened. "What do you think he might do?"

"Trump might not want to be seen doing anything himself, but he might persuade Vance to create more mischief in Pennsylvania."

"For sure it's the biggest swing state with twenty Electoral College votes."

"And it counts its ballots in the worst way."

"Huh?"

"After the polls close it can take up to five days to find out who won the election. Ballots cast before Election Day favor Democrats. So a Republican lead on election night can evaporate. And the longer the delay, the greater the opening for Vance—and maybe for Trump, and all sorts of bad actors to sow doubt about the outcome." I paused. "That's what happened in 2020. The Trumpsters cried fraud and the Stop-the-Stealers arrived in Washington for the wild J6 day that Trump had promised. And, after he riled them up, they attacked the Capitol."

"You think that Trump and Vance might do something like that?"

"I think they're thinking about it right now."

ELECTION ECHOES

The six of us gathered around Jackson and Margot's television screen switching between the CNN and Fox election night broadcasts. And here, right now, was CNN

"Kamala's win seems predestined," I said.

"The Trumpster so-called likely voters stayed home," said Ashleigh.

"So the popular vote is an overwhelming victory—"

"—and even with the Pennsylvania votes to come, she's already handily improving on the Biden 2020 electoral win."

"She's a breath away from a win," said Ashleigh

"For sure it's Kamala's night," said Margot.

"And there is," said Byrne. "North Carolina has just put her over the top."

Our applause was also echoed in the streets beyond our picture windows.

"As expected, surely," said Jackson. "I mean, did anyone ever think that anyone who voted for Biden in 2020 would switch and vote for the former guy?"

I grinned. "I'm sure Trump will share some kind and healing words in his acceptance of the results," I said.

"He's a loser now for sure," said Jackson.

"Big-time!" said Hassan.

"I rather doubt that he'll show up," said Jackson. "He'll likely be scheming for ways to turn this thing around."

"Yeah," said Hassan. "But how's he gonna make anything stick."

"The devil looks after his own," said Byrne.

He'd hardly uttered those words, when the screen dissolved to a shot of Vance front and center in the middle of what seemed a not-so-hastily arranged crowd of Trumpsters. His wide eyes peered from a MAGA cap, his torso encased in a black leather jacket over a red-checkered shirt, his right hand gripped a bullhorn as he declared, in his best redneck imitation, a Republican win in Pennsylvania. He raised his left fist, primped to full height, and delivered his next words in a more upmarket tone "As a proud member of the United States Senate," he said, "*I cannot—and we must not—sit by as yet another election is stolen from us. So stop the counting* of the ballots right now," he cried. "*Yeah, Stop it Now—or We Will Fight! Fight! Fight!*" He motioned his followers to join his chant. And so they did. "*We Will Fight! Fight! Fight! We Will Fight! Fight! Fight!* "And make no bones about it," said Vance, producing a snub-nosed revolver from his jacket and nodding expectantly to his followers. Unfortunately for him, though most were carrying steel pipes or shillelaghs, only several were armed with what looked like hunting rifles. Vance effected a threatening tone. "*And we're gonna march right in and close the counting down right now,*" he said. In that moment, a local sheriff and a couple of dozen police armed officers emerged from the shadows.

"What's going on here?" said the sheriff in a gruff but not entirely unpleasant tone. He glanced to Vance, then cast a studious eye over the Trumpsters. "I mean I hope we don't have to arrest anyone for, uh, disturbing the peace."

Upon those words, the Trumpsters sullenly folded their weapons into their jackets. "A great night for absolutely everyone," said the sheriff, still holding his ground.

"Yeah, maybe," said Vance's lieutenant, as his ragtag herd of followers sheepishly disappeared into the cool night air.

Jackson hit a button on the remote and switched to Fox's silver-haired anchor. "Vice presidential candidate JD Vance has just called for a civil uprising to halt the count of ballots in the Pennsylvania election," said the announcer. He paused as someone slipped him a note. "Hmm... We now have former president Donald Trump online from his Mar-a-Lago headquarters"… Clad in a MAGA cap, blue suit jacket, white shirt and red tie, Trump appeared on the screen, his blue eyes glaring out from within the trifling white circles bereft of orange suntan lotion. He morphed into a strongman pose. "I'm calling for a *national* uprising to protest the *travesty* of the continued counting of the ballots in so many of the *swing states* that we have *already* won. We won them *fairly and squarely*. And, just as surely as *Biden–Harris* have *weaponized* the Justice Department against me—*me*, personally, *ME!* As you know—as *everyone* knows actually—*corrupt* New York prosecutors and an absolutely *crooked* judge *commanded* a totally *immoral* jury to find me—*ME!*"—he tapped his heart—"*wrongfully* guilty of a felony. So, like I said, I'm calling on MAGA *patriots* and"—he flashed a momentarily benign smile—"*blessed Christians*—for a *national* uprising." Trump's image dissolved from the screen and this time a salt-and-pepper haired anchor stepped up to the plate. "That was a call to action from our former president Donald J. Trump." He glanced to a glass table of Fox pundits. "So what do we think?"

"Enough," said Jackson. He switched back to CNN and froze the screen. "So what do *we* think," he said with a smile.

"Not sure," said Hassan.

"It's the beginning of an ending," I said. "And it'll come with a whimper not a bang."

"Trump might still have tricks to play," said Margot.

"He always does," said Ashleigh.

"It ain't over till the final play," said Hassan."

"The Donald's leadership mantle is in tatters," said Jackson. "But let's see what happens when Judge Merchan passes sentence."

"One way or another, the devil looks after his own."

As it all turned out, Byrne was right.

PART FOUR

"The graveyards are full of indispensable men."

Charles de Gaulle

TRANSPARENT INVITATION

Jackson called as I was turning in that night. "I have some potential good news," he said. "My Fox contact says in the interest of transparency, the powers that be are keen to have an eclectic group of citizens attend the Merchan sentencing. Unfortunately I have a board meeting that morning so I can't be there. But, as you may recall, I originally told them that you and Byrne are dedicated Christians, so you're both already on their list. I just need to know whether you might care to join the gathering of public citizens who'll be meeting in the courtroom at nine in the morning."

I called Byrne and shared the news. "It will be an historic day for sure," he said. "I could get there after officiating at an early church service." He paused. "But I'm sure you'll already be inside the courtroom." He drew a sigh. "Perhaps I could arrive outside the courtroom, check the crowd reaction and catch the reports of the various television announcers—then later, we could meet up and share notes."

A black-robed archangel descended into my dream and pointed to a trailing crimson banner upon which emerald green letters spelled out a message. I looked closely. The words were in Latin. But before I could make sense of anything, the letters faded.

COLD COMFORT

I woke early and clad myself in the uniform of my charcoal suit—sans flag-pin—white shirt, blue tie, dark socks, and leather-soled, black wingtip shoes. I grabbed a full bacon-and-egg-breakfast at the eatery on the corner of 75th Street, then took the IRT train to the Brooklyn Hall Station.

To my surprise, on the walk to the Manhattan criminal court building, save for the usual traffic and some scattered clusters of pro and anti Trumpers, most of whom were joshing with each other, the streets were mostly normal. So much for the idea that an army of locked and loaded Trumpsters would upend their leader's sentencing.

I arrived at The Manhattan Criminal Court building at just after a quarter to nine. Barricaded inside, were a phalanx of New York's leather-jacketed, armed and truncheon-wielding police officers. Video cameras had been set up under an awning, apparently reserved for members of the press. I stepped into the building's lobby, and was met by a courteous official, who, after checking my ID, directed me to take the elevator to the fifteenth floor.

I immediately grasped why some people called the windowless courtroom cold, dingy, and unbefitting of hosting the criminal trial and conviction, and, now, the sentencing, of a former United States president. To be fair, the building is eighty years old so climate control is limited and courtroom reporters said temperature was not as icy as Trump had claimed. And Judge Merchan had noted that he preferred his courtroom a little cold, rather than too hot. I was directed to a seat in the back row of the attendees. Three rows were in front of mine, then, apparently, a row for members of the media. In front of that was seating for the defendant and his attorneys, ideally placed to gaze up at the judge's bench, which was set between two upright American flags, and, high on the wall behind the judge, the multi-colored New York State seal.

With time to spare I fell to ruminating. Whatever was I doing here? Had the universe itself dropped me into the maelstrom of events that led me to be sitting in this courtroom. And if so, why? No. The universe itself was surely just a dream. Or maybe an amalgam of random happenstances? *It is what it is,* as Zen Buddhists are fond of saying. But Trump himself used that same quote as a defence for doing nothing when Covid struck. A more practical philosophy might be that if we don't like the life we're living that we should create a better one. In my head I reread the lines from Hamlet just before he headed off to lose his life in an ill-fated duel. '*There is special providence in the fall of a sparrow: if it be now, is not to come; if it be not to come, it will be now; if it be not now, yet it will come-the readiness is all.*' Yes, of course, the readiness is all.

When I awoke from my reveries the courtroom was already packed with people, among them of reporters, sketch artists, and members of the public. Manhattan District Attorney Alvin Bragg and three aides were seated in the front row of the public gallery. And Trump was at the door. Flanked by three charcoal-suited lawyers, he primped to full height, tapped his red tie, then ambled from the doorway, and, as he had done so many times before, lowered himself into his swivel, golden-oak, jury-arm chair. So this was the fellow Jackson called the Donald. He seemed to have shrunk in stature. He glanced momentarily backwards apparently to check the crowd. His combover was been dyed a fainter, grayer, more becoming shade, and his face was paler than I expected. He swung back again to face the bench, and as far as I could tell, set his elbows on the desk, clasped his hands together, hunched forward, and assumed his Clockwork Orange mugshot glare. I could not help but wonder whether he was wearing a diaper beneath his is ample blue jacket, but I detected no strange aroma, which, given the dankness of the courtroom, was unsurprising.

"All rise!" We stood. His robes flowing behind him, Judge Julian Merchan strode from his chambers, swept into the courtroom, and descended to his bench beneath the justice seal, and between two unfurled American flags that had graced countless criminal trials. He seemed younger than I had expected, younger than Trump anyway, but as with some film noir movie stars—a bespectacled Humphrey Bogart came to mind—ageless, too. Given Trump's apparent hatred for tawny immigrants I pondered the irony of Judge Merchan's immigrant status. He arrived in America at age six, became a naturalized citizen, was the first member of his family to go to college, and, now, before my very eyes, was the first judge to ever pass sentence on a US President. As on a mission, he coolly welcomed us, then segued into calling Trump's lead attorney, Todd Blanche, to offer a statement.

Blanche stepped forward and turned his eyes upward to the Judge. "I need to note for the record that my client, Donald John Trump, has been the victim of Biden-Harris weaponized justice, and has been denied his right of free speech by the action of this court in imposing an illegal gag-order that made it impossible to conduct a free and fair presidential election, and which highlights the good-faith of my client in attending here today, for this so-called sentencing."

As he spoke, I fell to wondering how any lawyer could sell his tongue to Trump. Everyone has to find a way to survive, of course. So the lack of money—or, for greedy sinners, enough of it—is the root of all evil, and, as in the priesthood, the legal profession is a mixed bag of devils and saints. The saints are scholars, writers, logical, rational minds who enjoy the philosophy and application of law, but all too often wind up in the poor house. Unfortunately, the legal 'profession' also attracts narcissistic pathological liars who feed the avarice by getting guilty clients off. So, for them anyway, the way to make crime pay 'enough' is to join the greedy devils telling lies to help like-minded clients cheat the system. So, as we existential psychologists might say, no one chooses evil because it is evil; we merely mistake it for happiness and the pot of gold at rainbows end.

"My client is in the process of appealing this fake conviction to the Supreme Court of the United States. We affirm his right to enjoy free citizenship, and request that the court delay sentencing until that Supreme Court decision has been duly handed down."

"So noted," said Judge Merchan. He directed his next words to Trump. "Do you, Mister Trump, have anything you would like to add?" he asked. Blanche shared a whisper with Trump and they both stood. Trump paused as if uncertain of where exactly to direct his attention. He turned his head upwards in the direction of the judge and semi-primped. Was he looking for a camera and a gleaming light atop the Judicial forehead? Trump's words came so softly that I strained to hear them. "I'm a very innocent man." he said. He raised what seemed to me to be a feeble fist "As you heard my lawyer say,"—he tightened his knuckles and warily pumped his hand —"we shall take this fight to the Supreme Court of the United States of America"—he drew a sigh—"and we shall win." He paused, then on a nod from the Judge, he and Blanche lowered themselves back into their oaken chairs.

I'm not sure of his exact words, but Judge Merchan read from a lengthy recitation of the facts of the case. Then, glancing up, he spoke directly to Trump. "I am mindful of the fact that you appear before me as a citizen with no prior arrests or convictions. Your probation officers have also assured me that any risk of your engaging in any such further crime is minimal. I am also well aware that you are a former president of the United States of America. I also note that you have been held in contempt of this court by violating your gag-order. Most crucially, you have shown neither remorse nor contrition for the crimes of which you have been convicted by a jury of your peers. Any ordinary citizen who came before this court having been convicted of these felonies and contemptuous acts would receive a jail sentence of at least six months. I find no reason to treat this case any differently. Accordingly, the sentence of this court is that you are herewith sentenced serve six months in a New York correctional facility, effective immediately." Upon those words, as if by magic, three burly uniformed officers appeared and surrounded and handcuffed Trump and led him out of the courtroom. "I hereby declare this sentencing closed," intoned Judge Merchan, thudding his mahogany gavel into its tray. With minimal murmuring we all rose and stood in silence, as Judge Merchan clasped his notes to his chest, gathered his robes and flowed back into his private chambers. As we filed out court I thought I caught sight of Goebbels. The gait was the same, but the cloth-cap and sunglasses didn't match the fitted charcoal overcoat and a gray silk scarf. He'd have been here to join the entourage escorting Trump back home. Nice try, but out of luck.

I was dazed as I got pulled into what almost seemed a conga line led by anxious reporters intent upon descending down into the street to announce the historic news that a former United States president was in the custody of the New York Department of Corrections, and on his way to jail. Even now, in the hallway outside the courtroom, cheering and jeering could be heard from the street below from what sounded to be small gatherings of Trump supporters and detractors had gathered. The crowded elevator opened into the lobby where a television camera had been set up. Trump's lawyers, flanked by a smattering of his most ardent supporters nervously assembled to one side and waited. The rest of us were ushered to a vantage point behind a barricade.

Todd Blanche, grim faced, and clutching a note card, stepped forward. "This has been a bad day for American justice and for our entire nation." He glanced to his cue card and back. "A *very* bad day." He seemed about to say a whole lot more, but checked himself. "As you know, this entire case, including the verdict and sentencing, are being appealed to the Supreme Court of the United States." He folded his notes, turned, and led his entourage out the side door.

I met up with Byrne inside of the double barricaded avenue. As my eyes became accustomed to the midday sun, I took in the scene. If Trump had been expecting an angry revolution akin to the J6 storming of the Capitol, he'd have been woefully disappointed. Yes, there were scattered groups of Trump supporters in their starred and striped T-shirts and regalia, some of whom were waving placards. But, there were also as many Trump detractors. In fact, they all—mostly all, anyway— seemed remarkably good-natured, and to my eye, seemed to be joshing with one another.

"A truly historic day." Byrne said it as if he couldn't quite believe it. "Our former president is on his way to jail." He glanced backward and waved his arm over the near to empty street. "And it has all happened, as British Airways likes to say, with a minimum of fuss."

"At least not in Manhattan," I said.

"You were in the room where it happened,"—he half smiled—"what was *that* like?"

"I'm still processing it," I said.

He paused a moment. Maybe Byrne was mulling it, too. "Jackson and Margot have invited us to share a drink in their apartment. Hassan will be there, too. I'm sure that whatever is happening throughout the nation will feature on their television screen."

We sat around the coffee table. "I'm recording the news," said Jackson. "So we can play that later. I'm just wondering, as always, what we just thought of what went down today." He paused. "Let me get my two-cents worth out of the way."

Margot grinned. "Typical man," she said. "Always wants to go first."

"Not always," said Jackson. "So I defer to your opinion."

"He had it coming," she said. "He was a petulant child who needed a lesson in discipline, so I'm happy that it all caught up with him."

"He might just do all right in prison," said Hassan.

"If he truly is a leader," said Jackson, "he'll have followers, and he'll know how to win them over."

"He's famous and he's rich," said Hassan. Most guys in jail are kinda fond of that."

"Indeed," said Jackson. So they'll flatter him and he'll give them money—all outside the prison walls, of course."

"If that doesn't work," said Hassan, "they'll subtly threaten him."

"I don't envy his situation," said Jackson, "but I'm sure he'll find ways to help them help him to survive." He glanced to me. ""And how did Trump seem to you?"

My brain replayed Trump's courtroom presence. "He seemed to have shrunk," I said. "His hair seemed grayer, his face paler." Byrne was paying close attention. "He let his lawyer do most of the talking. Then, with some prodding, he accepted the judge's invitation to say something before the sentence reading." I reflected on that moment. "He waved his fist said he'd fight to the end. But he didn't seem as cocky as usual. I got the impression his heart wasn't truly in it."

Byrne mulled my words, then smiled benignly and fixed me with a steady gaze. "What you just described," he whispered, "is the shell of a person whom the devil has left behind." He drew a long sigh. "Donald Trump is no longer possessed by Satan. He's on his own now. And he's woefully unsure of what he's doing or where he's heading."

Hassan glanced to his wristwatch. "He might be heading to his cell right now," he said.

"Donald Trump has always been inside a prison," said Byrne. "And now he's free to become what he has already become; one more lost soul in the land of the living dead."

Jackson hit the remote to replay the news.

None other than NBC's Lawrence O'Donnell appeared. "I always fancy this fellow's hint of an Irish accent," said Margot. "And his insights, too, of course." We listened in silence, as the esteemed reporter delivered measured tones...

"On this day of 24 November 2024 Donald J. Trump, assuming his defiant Mafia Don pose, but looking a little worse for wear, appeared in Judge Juan Merchan's courtroom to hear his sentence in the matter of his Hush-Money case and his thirty-four felony convictions by a jury of his peers in a New York State Court. As expected Judge Merchan read out a lengthy summation the case, noting that the payoff of a porn star by a civilian prior to a presidential election was a purely private act, and, since the relevant crime was committed in New York State, there was no viable argument for the defendant to rely on any other court. Judge Merchan then listened with apparent equanimity to remarks by Donald Trump's lead lawyer, Todd Blanche. Then, after noting that the defendant was a former United States president with no prior convictions, Judge Merchan went on to observe that in the course of administering this case, he had to hold Donald Trump in contempt for violating a gag-order, and that the defendant had shown no admission of guilt or expression of remorse for any of his criminal activity. The Judge noted that any other such citizen would be serving serious jail time, and so he sentenced Citizen Trump to serve six months of jail time, effective immediately. So saying, he banged his gavel, gathered his robes and exited the courtroom." He paused. "And so, it seems, to this reporter, anyway, that Federal Judge Juan Merchan has affirmed that no citizen of these United States is above the law."

The television screen dissolved to the streets of Pennsylvania. Groups of diehard Trumpster's were on the streets. But, so too, quietly in the background, were leather-jacketed sheriffs and police officers. As far as I could tell, none of the Trumpster's were armed.

Jackson, doused the volume. "It's like, as I think I said before, akin to a 'reality' show," he said. "But this time the Donald isn't present to lead the crowd, so the television cameras are scanning the scene instead of focusing upon him." He paused. "His cultists might not know it but the Donald's show is over. By the time he gets out of jail, and even now, his audience is fading fast. America is back to normal."

"Yeah, normal—whatever that is," said Hassan.

In my dream an angel descended and hovered astride a bridge dividing paradise from hell. I was at the gates of heaven and Donald Trump was at the gates of hell. The angel seemed to recognize me and blessed me with a prayer. I wanted to respond but did not know what to say. In any case my mouth was blocked with ancient scrolls. The angel turned to Donald, produced a gleaming knife, sliced into his heart, and, wickedly laughing, Fred Trump emerged. And I awoke.

THE STING IN THE TAIL

Why in the name of hell would I dream of Donald Trump's father? *A dream that has not been analyzed is like a letter that has not been opened.* Did Freud say that? No matter. It's true. My unconscious was sending me a letter. I searched my memory. Fred Trump was cruel and ruthless. I went online and searched that paterfamilias. So, to curb his devilish son, Fred delivered that thirteen-year-old boy to a military school with a notoriously brutal 'anger management' program. "They have this wonderful mission statement," said an anguished parent to the *New York Times*, "but the reality is that it's a torture chamber in there. The kids are in charge. It's *The Lord of the Flies.*" Indeed. In 1984 a student had been at the academy for nine days when he awoke in his bed with a broken nose, a missing tooth, and blood pouring from his face. While sleeping, he had been clubbed over the head with a bicycle lock inside a tube sock, a practice known at the school as a 'lock n sock.' His attacker was a student officer overseeing her son in the anger management program. "But that doesn't make him a bad kid," said the program commandant. The parents' lawyer said another dozen incidents surfaced over the decade. And the local police chief warned school officials about their failure to report possible criminal activity.

Donald Trump's yearbook noted that being a "Ladies' Man" was his "greatest achievement." A fellow student also told a reporter, "There wasn't a lot of time for girls... but he was a good-looking guy... so it was appropriate." My mind raced. I've gotten into the habit of reading potential underlying meanings into words and phrases. So, given the brutality of these anger management classes, I stuck on the epithet, *ladies-man.* Was this an intentional double entendre? And what about the line, "It was appropriate."? *Appropriate?* My mind flashed back to the conversation with the producer of *The Apprentice*. He'd said that even at forty years of age, Trump was incontinent. But, if so, why? Given the apparently unlicensed brutality of the Military Academy anger management classes had Trump been the victim of unthinkable physical and sexual abuse? If so, perhaps incontinence had resulted from penetrations into more than his heart and soul. That would explain the apparent sarcasm in the "Ladies-Man" accolade, and the irony in the word "appropriate."

It might also clarify the apparent evil of Donald Trump's behavior. He'd unconsciously spent just about every moment of his life attempting to get even with everyone who had done him wrong. For these wretched lords of flies, he had grandiosely promoted himself as a business genius. For them, he had shown the world a gift for demeaning and insulting virtually every person he encountered. A racist and misogynist, he unleashed precisely those primitive emotions in his followers. But no woman—wife, whore, or stranger grabbed by the groin—could ever satisfy his lust to get even with the hateful father who delivered him to the young men who had so cruelly reshaped him in those so-called anger management classes. Fred Trump probably caught wind of the methods employed to release his son's demons. If so, the reckless promotion—and ongoing financial rescues—of the malevolent son he molded make perfect sense. That would also explain why Donald Trump was susceptible to the flattery of authoritarian father-surrogates. Putin, the criminal master-spy, had surely understood all of this, and groomed the woebegone son to effect havoc on the USA. But was Trump truly evil? Byrne would say so. And what about the New York Military Academy? Was that, like maybe the Vatican itself, an incorrigible institution? *It is what it is.* And so is the world. And thank heaven for existential psychology is what I say.

AMERICA

It's a secular celebration, so I love Thanksgiving almost as much as Donald Trump hates Taylor Swift. And so, with Byrne, Ashleigh, and Hassan, I delightedly accepted the invitation of Jackson and Margot to join them for Thanksgiving dinner, which, by sheer good luck, happened just two days after the jailing of our former president.

Margot had prepared and roasted a perfect turkey dinner replete with Brussels sprouts, sweet potato, and cream corn. Jackson carved and slipped the slices onto a antique ivory serving dish and set it on the dining table for us to help ourselves, which we did, and then, with an overlay of cranberry sauce and sparkling conversation, politely devoured.

Margot delivered the pumpkin pie and cream.

"So, I said"—for the second time, I might add—"now that we have a new president, most of America is celebrating Thanksgiving." Sensing a sweet aroma. I glanced to the coffee table where Margot had set a blaze of red roses and white lilies among seasonal greens.

"The Donald is surely gone for good," said Jackson, with a sigh.

"He might be eating a turkey of his own right now," said Hassan.

"Indeed; they serve Thanksgiving turkey in jail," said Ashleigh.

"Big time," said Hassan.

"All that worrying for nothing," said Jackson. He sliced the apple pie into eight pieces and passed them around.

"America isn't smarter than any other nation." I sipped my Chardonnay. "Our strength is our ability to finally fix whatever goes wrong.

"But nothing happens on its own," said Margot.

"America is a large friendly dog in a small room," said Hassan. "Every time it wags its tail it knocks over a chair.

"We connect the dots by looking backwards," said Byrne.

"But we have to trust that the dots will make sense of the way ahead," said Ashleigh.

"You got to trust in something; gut, destiny, life, karma, jazz, whatever," said Hassan.

"Jazz?" said Byrne.

"It connects us to our earlier selves," I said.

"And our better selves to come," said Margot.

"Music is moonlight in the gloomy night of life," said Jackson.

"I hear a choir and know there's a God," said Byrne.

"Whither goest thou, America, in thy shiny car in the night?" I said.

"If you own a home with wheels and several cars without, you just might be a redneck," said Hassan.

"We've given ourselves over to magical thinking," I said. "The better way to deal with other people's darkness is to know your own."

"That's why so many believe in fairy tales," said Ashleigh.

"The reality of supernatural forces is something most people experience in every day," said Byrne.

"We live in a rainbow of chaos," said Ashleigh.

"We all have hunches we can't prove," I said.

"If there's a country that has committed unspeakable atrocities in the world, it has to be the USA," said Hassan.

"Until we get equality in education, we won't have an equal society," said Ashleigh. "My dream is of a place and a time where America will once again be seen as the last best hope of earth."

"The best argument against democracy is a five-minute conversation with the average voter," said Jackson.

"Some people have been privileged for so long, that equality feels like oppression," said Hassan.

"The best way to predict the future is to create it," said Jackson.

"America is the land of the second chance," said Hassan.

"It's not the harvest we reap; it's the seeds we plant," said Margot.

With the pie all gone, I glanced to Jackson and Margot. "You guys intrigue me," I said. "I mean, why ever did you come to America?"

"And stay and become citizens," said Hassan.

"It might help if you know that in New Zealand the images of the monarch became indelibly imprinted upon our childhood psyches," said Jackson.

"Before any public event, including the screening of local movies," said Margot—"

"—we all sprang to our feet, stood to attention before some Technicolor image of the royal ruler, and sang for God to watch over that gracious and redeeming potentate," said Jackson. "A cult of sovereignty permeated our lives."

"Royal-family books were everywhere," said Margot.

"Peeping into the intimate images of these aristocrats they seemed more than merely people; they were authentic nobility... So becoming an American bequeathed us more than a sense of identity. It evoked an affinity with newfound fellow-citizens of all stripes, colors and hues.

"Ah yes, America, it's not so much a place as a state of mind," said Byrne.

"The only country deliberately founded on the very good idea that we inhabit a secular country where everyone is equal and entitled to an equal vote, and no one is above the law."

"Do you *feel* any different?" said Hassan.

Jackson grinned. "To be honest, sometimes I wake in

the middle of the night to the awesome realization that we've rejected the British Empire." He paused. "I'm just another nameless, vulgar American." He exchanged the grin for a benign smile. "But, yes, I do feel differently... I'm no longer stuck with the status quo. And anything I do to enhance it—my duty surely—will be welcomed. And whenever the steel gates lock me into my weekly prison classroom I feel a special new empathy with my putative scholars."

Hassan stepped into the warm smiles with a wide grin. "We were just asking," he said.

"Byrne unfolded a piece of paper. Listen up my friends," he said. "I found this quote from literary critic Bliss Perry." He read it aloud... "*No one can understand America with his brains. It is too big, too puzzling. It tempts, and it deceives.*" He drew a breath. "*But many an illiterate immigrant has felt the true America in his pulses before he ever crossed the Atlantic.*" He sighed. "*The descendant of the Pilgrims still remains ignorant of our national life if he does not respond to its glorious zest, its throbbing energy, its forward surge, its uncomprehending belief in the future, its sense of the fresh and mighty world just beyond today's horizon.*" He shared a look with Hassan. "*It beats with the pulse of this onward movement, because*"—Hassan completed the line—"*it is full of this laughing and conquering fellowship–*" Jackson jumped in, "Kamala would love that line." Byrne finished the sentence "*—and undefeated faith.*"

"That was quite a Thanksgiving," said Hassan.

We raised a toast, touched our glasses, and shared the moment.

I slept like a baby that night, then awoke refreshed and looking forward to Inauguration Day and a whole new era.

CODICIL

"Fiction reveals truth that reality obscures."
Ralph Waldo Emerson

TRUTH AND FICTION
A Codicil by author John Wareham

In June of 2024 I recalled Picasso's observation, "art is a lie that reveals the truth." If so, then fiction is the truth inside the lie. Inspired by these thoughts, even though I'm a secular, apolitical pragmatist, I set to penning *Exorcizing the Donald*.

To disclose the reality of truth in fiction, a writer must take readers on a credible journey of the heart and mind within a reimagined world. Fiction also insists on pursuing truth to the bitter end. And so, the exorcism scene in this book—where I had originally imagined the story would end—merely opened a basement stairway into even darker place, where, to my novelist eye, bitter truths were buried.

Rightly or wrongly, I chose to release this book in the first week of October 2024. So, among other prophecies, perched on the narrator's shoulder, readers observe 5 November 2024 election day street scenes. They also enter the chilly 26 November 2024 New York courthouse of Federal Judge Juan Merchan and share what happens before, during, and after his final judgement in the New York 'Hush-Money' sentencing hearing.

But what if these metafictional narrations turn out to be mistaken? My answer as a novelist is that whatever readers choose to believe is the only reality that matters. They'll know how events turned out and judge my novel accordingly. With luck, even if I didn't get everything right, they'll merely shrug and believe my novel to be a satisfying work of the imagination that perhaps ought to be true.

AUTHOR

John Wareham is an organizational leadership consultant and keynote speaker. He is also chair and chief of the Eagles Foundation, a not-for-profit that identifies and develops leaders from within the prison population. He is widely published, in non-fiction, fiction, and poetry. He can be contacted via his official Authors Guild website. https//www.johnwareham.com

THANKS

My very special thanks to Margaret
King, mercurial principal of The Flatiron
Literary Agency; to Craig Rubano, Richard
Habersham III, Don Brash, Dean Wareham
and John Weber, the inspiring chief of
Welcome Rain Publishers, for his ever-
generous support and sage advice.

John Wareham's Work Also Includes

METAFICTION
Chancey On Top.
The President's Therapist.
Exposed.

POETRY
Sonnets for Sinners.
How to Survive a Bullet
to the Heart.

NON FICTION
How to Break Out
of Prison.

The Breakout Plan.

Talking Your Way
to the Top.

Wareham's Way.

Zap Your Inner Demons
and create the life of your dreams

All prisons are mental prisons. They lock from the inside and you hold the key, so only you *can* let yourself out—but you *can* let yourself out....

THE EAGLES CIRCLE FOUNDATION INC.
PODCAST SERIES

Available now on Apple, Spotify, or via www.eaglesgather.org

The Breakout Plan Podcast Series

Pulitzer Prize Nominee
Listeners in 400+ Cities

JOHN WAREHAM

A Kiwi Catcher in the Rye?*

This startling new work pushes the memoir envelope, and makes clear why the *New York Times* observed, "John Wareham has the cool, clear eyes of a seeker of wisdom and truth."

With candour, irreverence and wit, Wareham reveals the surreal, swirling inner life of a child with a crippling stutter, whose emotional, sexual and spiritual journeys pass through rivers of despair in New Zealand, to a flood of enlightenment in New York.

"Brilliant and compelling ... reveals the mind and heart of boyhood ... touched me deeply."

—**Brian O'Dea,**
author of *HIGH: Confessions of an International Drug Smuggler.*

*
"Unputdownable... a passionate, Kiwi *Catcher in the Rye.*"
—*Charles DeFanti,*
Kean University Professor of Literature

Welcome Rain Publishers, LLC
 New York

A Love Triangle for the ages.

Just as his big-time dreams seem about to come true, Chandler Haste glances into the rear view mirror of the limousine bearing him across Manhattan's Triboro Bridge, and catches the reflection of a scorching affair from his past overleaping oceans to engulf him.

"**Dazzling** . . . a delicious literary bonbon . . . **ranks among the finest novels.**"—*New York Observer* "**Inspired** . . . philosophically savvy, **hilarious,** whimsical." — *Kirkus Reviews* "**Stunning** . . . an ardent . . . an affecting . . . assured exploration of moral quandaries."—*Publishers Weekly* "**Poetic gold!** The finest contemporary showcasing of the sonnet form."—Charles Defanti, professor of literature, and author of *The Wages of Expectation; the Biography of Edward Dahlberg.* "**Shattering** . . . Those who find their wisdom in **wild and witty** packaging will love *Chancey* . . . **deeply moving.**"—Bernard Berkowitz, Ph.D. author of *How to Be Your Own Best Friend* "**Magnificent . . . racy and contentious** . . . literary and erudite . . . **profound and moving.** Captures the inner conflicts of conscience and provides **authentic insights** into the struggles of upward strivers."— Harry Levinson, clinical psychologist, Harvard Medical School.

Welcome Rain Publishers, LLC

New York